A Prisoner behind the Bars of Time

A Prisoner behind the Bars of Time

A novel

By

Zeina Ibrahim Jradi

What life gives us, fate instead takes it away in the form of pain, since it is impossible for giving to be equal to not giving, as long as the game of life is a journey in which there is a tear and a smile.

Zeina I. Jradi

Author's Dedication

When the remains of certain things are born within us... tendencies towards our decisions diverge.

When they kill the love in our hearts... they become the jailers and the executioners, so that fingers become the bars of prison... and paths toward ourselves become unreachable...

A prisoner behind the bars of time...A tragedy of a woman whose fate changed her destiny... and eliminated the joy hidden under the gown of her adolescence...and her dreams... A woman who was kidnapped by a selfish man to be his slave.

Memories of a lifetime... which were choked with sorrow... where loneliness had stolen their vitality and took away their beauty...

To every woman whose Eve has rebelled... revolted... persecuted... imprisoned... fell in love... and broken. I dedicate my novel to a heart who is still looking for another heart that beats normally.

Author's Word

I worked hard to reveal myself on paper... I sewed a gown for the letters through my feelings. The character of the hero in the details of my novel was clear... I stole sorrow and happiness from the shadows of the horizon...

I always waited for her when the pictures flowed into my memory...and she used to come unexpectedly...worrying me... occupying my days and evenings... and lighting up the narration eagerness within me...

She was taking me involuntarily with her... waiting me by the love of leaving away, and by the blowing of torments in her life...She made me tired by revealing her pain, her destiny, and the game of time along her story. I imagined her as pictures... maybe.

I imagined her as words, meanings and events... maybe.

However, every time she got frustrated, she used to throw away the sorrows and fly again like a phoenix.

She became real; she was born from imagination, reality and pain. Her events were scattered in all directions.

A prisoner behind the bars of time...

A novel that proves the game of fate, and a pen used to make decisions by a woman who has been deprived of making decision... The narration of events, although well-crafted by imagination, remains real evidence for a story of a woman who has been tired of time.

Zeina I. Jradi

> "The silence that follows a massive disaster is the most peaceful sound you can hear on the surface of the world". - Elif Shafak

Her dreams were so young to go beyond her uniform of school… She was still growing like a rose bud which needs the dew to bloom. Although hatred is detested, but mercy is also permissible for those on Earth…Everything was smartly prepared and ready but waiting her arrival from school. There was the Sheikh, the witnesses, the family and the unexpected surprise: **the GROOM**.

"Please Mom…"A smothered voice of a child.

But, who is she calling??The forbiddance has occurred, and this marriage has already made under the guise that: "marriage is a shelter" for you and for every girl my daughter.

The girl replied with a slaughtered voice: "But Mom… I don't know him, and even all of you don't know him… Is it sufficient for the husband to be an expatriate in order to be the right man!!!"

- "Come on, tell the Sheikh: You are my proxy…" A firm phrase said by the mother.

However, the girl insisted on refusing this deal…

The mother got angry… her face became gloomy and her features appeared to be completely changed. Owing to her furious reaction, she started telling rough words, threatening and intimidating, while she said: "If you don't talk, I will ask the guests to leave, then your punishment will be difficult and you know the rest".

To avoid the punishment, I gave into the inevitable and closed the deal…

- You are my proxy…

A sentence which I pronounced before the Sheikh, where the marriage was convened and the journey with the expatriate Adnan has begun…

This is a biography of a sixteen-year-old young girl, which started by a coercion whiff and did not end.

"Pain changes people, makes them trust less, think more, and isolate longer". - Gibran Khalil Gibran.

A hail of rain blocks the view and the sky is open over unfamiliar floods. This is the law of nature in Africa, endlessly torrential rain. As usual, loneliness prevails within me while waiting the return of Adnan, who never allows me to interfere with his privacy and his life. My job was only, to be a wife in front of people and to be an alternative maid for his home abroad. He stripped me of all my powers. I have nothing to do with money and requirements, and he is not even responsible for meeting my needs, except for a little food. This was the rule of my marriage or "my shelter" as imposed by my mother, and which was outside my dreams. As a teenager, I dreamed about things belonging to teenagers, but apparently, even the dream was not considered as my right. I was prisoned by his orders and detained in life. It was forbidden for me to meet anyone or to receive guests, since he believed that I may feel jealous from them or I shall dare to ask for something prohibited…

My mother implicated me in this trouble, and perhaps the worst thereof was if I dare and ask for a need, the insults quickly heaped upon me, and it may sometimes reach the limit of beating. However, the matter was not new to me, since I got used before to my mother's cruelty, so there was no difference between the past and the present, and the burden of Adnan remains unfairly lighter than what I was suffering.

Deep pain and a state of nausea without interruption.... What happened my God??! I may have been poisoned by food... But the pain is no longer tolerable. My intestine is about to rupture even though it is empty. I even can no longer drink water ... Days have passed while I was trying to cope with my pain, perhaps it may be dissipated by a little hot drink or by boiling the chamomile herb, but in vain, as vomiting does not stop even if I drink only water.

The pain aggravated as if the hoop was intensified upon a victim's neck, and I began to feel fainting cases from time to time, even my voice became choked, almost expressing my suffering. Adnan has been away from home for a long time, while I was alone, writhing like a chicken slaughtered from vein to vein. All traditional treatment methods failed me, and my body became cold like the bodies of the dead...Finally, Adnan arrived, as usual, angry and distracted, so I asked him to visit the doctor in order to inspect my case.

He replied sarcastically:

- Reduce food and have mercy on yourself, this is the result of greed.

I turned to him with a broken heart and said:

- This is what you come up with!? Is it due to food, or are you afraid to pay the doctor's examination and the medicine bill?

The response shocked him, so he hit me like a tough spiteful rapist. His reaction always broke you into pieces and he did not know mercy, as if he was taking revenge on himself for marrying me.

He was mentally ill without a doubt, complicated and with no humanity. His bad treatment was killing all the beautiful things for me, pouring out a lava of fire on my dreams, and making me suffocate. I was supposed to spend the honeymoon in a romantic and compassionate atmosphere full of tenderness, warmth and strong emotions that serve as a safe fort for every girl who is newly married and at a very early age...I remembered with every slap I was receiving from him, my mother's selfishness, her denial and backwardness, so the slaps were twice hit on my sick body.

I told him in a smothered voice:

9

- Adnan, Fear God, what is my sin with you? I am your wife now, and I am supposed to be a bride enjoying a honeymoon with her partner.

He replied:

- You came to my life as a disaster and your presence caused the complete change to it…. You are a disaster!!
- You are crazy ill

I said it with tizzy and fear.

He pounced on me like a beast pounces on its prey and he started hitting me randomly, while I was running around the corners of the house to escape from his madness. I had always repeated this expression as an orphan: Please… I beg you, I want to go back to Lebanon… I want to return to my parents… to my family.

The more I begged him, the more violent he became, until he lost control of himself, and I fell unconscious as if I had slipped out of my world and plunged into another world that I did not feel its existence, but was in a temporary coma.

When I regained consciousness and woke up from that condition, I opened my eyes to a thick-faced African woman, as if she was a lump of flesh trying to wake me up. At first, I thought I was just speculating about it as a dream, but I came back and realized a realistic fact that Adnan had sought help from this African woman for fear of being legally prosecuted with the issue of violence, and I also realized that the issue of violence against women in the African continent is one of the complicated issues that may lead a man to imprisonment, as in most countries.This African woman, I think, was the wife of a worker who works for him in the transportation company, and since he had fear that I would prosecute him before the police, he came with her to help me reduce my pain.

I wasn't allowed to call my family. I was imprisoned in a house whose rooms were almost taking my breath away and suffocating me, and its doors almost depriving me of the bloom of life. I was alone with my sadness, feelings, and foreignness We were a couple, each of us separated by great distances. He considered me as a piece of furniture, so he bought me to complete his home decor. He was a mysterious man and his appearance almost deceived you about his inner characteristics… He was a beast in the form of a human being.

I lived with my pain as the wound fuses after surgery, while the African woman "Rose" used to visit me from time to time, trying to treat me by traditional methods. The pain reduced in my intestines, but the nausea was getting worse, my body tended to be thin, my face looked pale, my steps became heavy and my

11

powers faded. Weeks have passed with this condition, and I was feeling upset day after day. I don't control myself from falling on the ground every time I tried to move in the house, since I am actually in a state of early conflict and disability. Rose's visits are the only savior that helps me and makes me feel I'm still alive.

What is the secret of this nausea? A question that I asked myself repeatedly, until I noticed a swelling in my belly and I knew about my pregnancy, and that there is a partner coming from the unknown who will share life with me.

- Adnan, it is time to know the truth.

I faced him with these words... He goggled his eyes and the features of his face were completely changed. However, his condition did not scare me, since I realized that death is the same, even if there are many reasons for it.

He rebuked me saying:

- Tell me what you have from the misfortunes.

I told him:

- It is not a misfortune... but a divine blessing.

He responded nervously and randomly, saying:

- I told you tell me what you have Elham, or??

I gave him a sarcastic look, as if I had warned him that your threat was no longer useful to me, and I told him:

- I am pregnant!

He froze in his place for seconds while wondering, and said:

- What…. Tell it one more time!

I told him coldly:

- I am pregnant, my dear husband…

His severe anger blew, and he seemed unable to control himself, as if I committed adultery against him. I cannot understand why he got married to me and wanted me a partner for his life? He does not want me to have a child who shall fill our life with joy, dispel all these disputes and make the distance between us much closer. My husband lost the mercy of hearts.

I had a terrible fear and even a horror that swept through my eyes whenever I looked at my appearance. My belly became swollen, many things began to change in me, and my skin became paler, as if I was practicing oppression over an innocent soul that had not seen the light yet…How difficult is the feeling of loneliness in a situation similar to mine, imprisoned in spirit and body, under the weight of a husband who raped my rights! Thoughts swung my feelings between the moments of darkness and the selfishness of a strict man. I used to be distracted sometimes by packing the birth bag, contemplating the clothes of an angel visitor, almost like baby clothes, tattered, fragile, almost worn out, since the father had never tasted mercy and sympathy, as if the visitor was his enemy. I prayed a lot that my strange visitor would be a breeze of mercy to this humble home, or a message of love that would restore warmth and familiarity to the hearts of its residents.

My days passed cold and painful, and I was tasting the bitter of life. My tears have not dried up from my pillow, my moments passed as eons, and I was submerged in a frightening loneliness. My heart can barely feel its intermittent beats while it was resisting against the smell of longing and missing which I was blowing therein for the touch of an affectious mother or the sympathy of a warm, nostalgic brother.

The last days of my pregnancy were like the unfairly dark winter nights in our house, and like the memories that are forgotten by a teenage girl who killed her dreams and left the school earlier. The zero hour rang.

The pains seeped into my thin body and I entered the stage of labor. It was a strange experience for me, and a serious pain where my screams sounded frightening. I was alone, spinning around like a rabid cat seeking salvation. I turn and rotate in two rooms that are said to be a marital home, and my only hope was that the eye of heaven from its above, would have mercy on my situation and would reduce the burden of my pain.

Minutes turned into hours, and my voice started to suffocate slowly, until my amniotic sac ruptured, "my water" broke, and I sank in a lake without knowing or realizing that the expected visitor could no longer wait. I broke the mask of fear and went out in a panic to the street, wandering between faces strange to me, among black passers-by, where my scream sounds like the bells of Eid. My steps were heavy and my body was unable to move, so strange faces looped around me like rings and their hearts were filled with mercy and compassion, while Adnan was absent, overwhelmed with his pleasures, and not caring whether I was living or dying.

The magnanimity increased after I lost consciousness. I opened my eyes while I was in the hospital among a group of angels of mercy.

For the first time, I feel safe, the storm of fear that swept me has subsided and I glimpsed in the amidst of my pain my mother's face, who had not bothered to ask about my condition since the day I left her home, the day she sold me to a man with whom she thought that my immigration to Africa is considered as a mine of inexhaustible money. I wondered about the feeling of motherhood, and my visitor was still kicking hard, calling for the moment to go out to life ...My mother's harshness slowed down the release process. Her looks, her voice, her insistence on completing the sale deal, all were like anesthetic needles in my body, and I felt tears in my eyeballs, so I raised my gaze to above, and whispered with a wounded voice, saying: "I gave you my soul, O Lord of the Worlds".

The pains of labor were like knives tearing me apart, and my screaming refused to be confined to the walls of the room, but it was seeking to penetrate the sky, asking for mercy from the Lord of the worlds. The faces were confused, the nurses were coming and going, like a beehive, and the doctor insisted on conducting a cesarean section to complete the birth process, which shall increase my sense of pain. My condition became very miserable and dangerous, so I entered into a struggle between life and death, and the events around me became almost empty of the hearing sense, until the doctor ordered to enter by an emergency situation to the operating room, in order to preserve my safety and the safety of the visitor, the angel who at any moment may open the door of the world widely and come to us.

For the first time, the soul leaves me stealthily. I see my body lying down, and around me a group of nurses waiting for the doctor to come in order to conduct a cesarean delivery. I was on the verge of death like a humiliated lonely person who needs affection, as if I was painting my funeral with a feather of my breath. The cold seeped into my body up to my extremities, and I remembered that dead people lose heat at the moment of their struggle and departing from life, to be corpses upon passing towards death. I lost focus on time and circumstance, and on all that I was suffering, so I fell into a paralyzed coma, in which I lost consciousness for a moment, then I came back to life again. Both hands of the doctor were pressing hard on my stomach while repeating, "Take a deep breath ... Push again hard ..."

I heard a voice screaming ... a voice that shook me from the bottom of my heart. He was soft and hot, as I felt him on my chest when I was semi-conscious, while the voice of the doctor creeps into my ears saying:

- Congratulations, my daughter, God has helped you not to carry out a caesarean section ... Here is your newborn with full health and wellness ...

The doctor almost finished his last sentence until I fell into a deep sleep... I plunged into a world that I don't remember at all, but what was left from my memory is the tragedy of a woman who is destined to taste the torment since her childhood.

Hours after hours have passed while I was drowned in a deep sleep, until the sunlight tickled my eyelids. I opened my eyes and my belly was still bloated.

I was afraid that what I suffered was just a nightmare, so I requested to see the doctor to ask him if I had given birth to my child or not yet, and if he operated a caesarean section or not. I started to touch my belly hoping to find the wound, so the doctor, who is of Arab origin, smiled and took two steps to me, then whispered, saying:

- Your delivery was so dangerous, you passed away for seconds…

The first thing I asked for was my child... My visitor who was coming from the basement of oppression and deprivation, and who was fed by torment and persecution, and by the cruelty of a ruthless father ...

The doctor took again two steps back, and whispered:

- They will bring you later your innocent angel, but now you need to rest.

I went back to my sleep, while the sun started to warm and my condition became fine. During my sleep, I heard the sound of ababy cart, so I opened my eyes in panic. The nurse was entering the room while she was pulling a cart with my little angel therein. My heart stopped beating for a second, and I felt a light penetrating me that no phrases could describe. Once the nurse bent down to hug him, I felt the beautiful moments of the motherhood. What a strange feeling for a mother who has not yet reached the age of seventeen, carrying in her hands a deposit that reveals the light of God in its features... Blessed be God for what He created ...His contours are like a mosaic, and his eyes ... I did not recognize them, since they were closed. I brought him close to my face, so I feel his breath as a nostalgic breeze that lit the fire of his presence in mine.

I contemplated the features of my angel visitor, and I found him in complete beauty. Blessed be God for this creature! I immediately decided to call him "Kamal" (perfection) hoping it would be perfect to fill the lost happiness in our home.

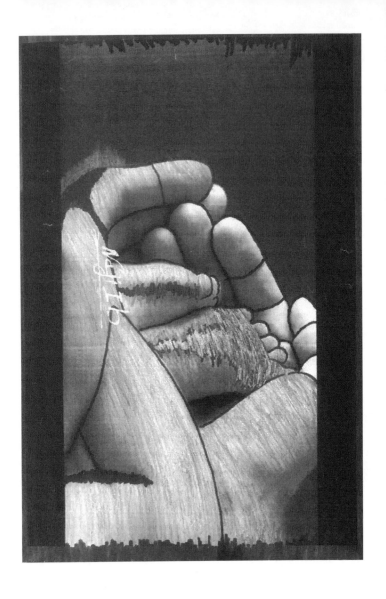

"The most beautiful moments of my happiness must always be mixed with a bit of sadness". - Dostoevsky

---

While I was overwhelmed by contemplating my visitor, the doctor entered the room again, but his features changed from the previous time, I tightened the baby to my chest ... I was afraid that something would happen to him, so he approached me until his face almost stuck my face, and he asked me:

- What is your name?

I felt as though I was in the presence of an intelligence man's investigation, so I told him:

- Elham.

He ordered the nurse who shared the room with us to put a bracelet on the baby's wrist on which she wrote the phrase: Kamal, the son of Elham.

My tragedy faded with the journey of labor, and I began to regain my focus and to recover my health ... While I was hugging the most precious thing that the Creator had given me, my son Kamal, I suddenly wake up from my sleep and wonder myself: Where is Adnan? Where is my husband? I called the nurses' room, and they came in a hurry wondering about what happened. I chose the face that I was relieved by its smile and affection, and

I gave her Adnan's address to tell him about my current situation and the arrival of Kamal.

I was waiting his coming to convene a new love treaty whose hero is my little angel…I was sure that his tenderness would melt in the eyes of this angel and he would be eager to touch his pure hands, for nothing is more wonderful than the innocence of children that saves us from the cruelty and brutality of life.

Adnan arrived late as usual, frowning his eyebrows and almost sparks of evil flying from his eyes. However, instead of congratulating me on safety and showing craving feelings of paternity to see his child, he was boiling blood, agitated, rebellious, menacing, and threatening a punishment, repeating:

- How?? How?? How do you do this heinous act Elham? Who taught you the fundamentals of decency and obedience? How do you get out of your home without telling me what happened? Do you think I am a man with no word?

He was babbling hateful words as if he was throwing burnt oil at me, trying to distort the feelings of my motherhood and my joy. Despite my suffering, the groan of pain returned to my chest, so I screamed:

- Enough … What kind of men are you? Don't you fear God, for I was close to death ... Where is mercy in your heart???

He stared at me saying:

- Pretexts and lies… I understand you well Elham…

My respect to him has gone, so I looked at him with hatred, saying:

- May God forgive you ... Hearts that do not know mercy will undoubtedly know love.

I raised the angel visitor between my hands to his face, and shouted at him:

- Take… your son Kamal…

He turned his back as if this angel was a bastard, not of his own flesh and blood.

I don't care, as long as I have my baby, I have someone who lifts off my shoulders Adnan's fears, oppression, hate and spite. I became a partner to a spirit that came to me from above ... from the highest ... from the Lord of the worlds ... and in a flash, my life has become divided into two parts:

The first part: Me, then me, then me, and the second part: Kamal, then Kamal, then Kamal. I was an ignorant mother who did not know how to take care of the infant or how to deal with him and how to carry him between the arms, and she did not know anything about how to breastfeed. I was a simple mother, not yet seventeen years old. Her mother forced her to become a mother at such a young age, so that her adolescence would change into maturity, forget teenage games and play with heavy responsibilities. I was getting lost in the purity of his eyes, wiping my tears from his palms and repeating to him:

- Forgive me Mom... I am still in the elementary class of motherhood school.

When the Lord of the Worlds honors you, do not ask him about the secret of his generosity! The nurse with an attractive smile, who I knew her name later as "Mary," volunteered and hugged Kamal in her arms to teach me the best ways to embrace the baby, then she started teaching me lessons on how to breastfeed ...I was eager to know how the mother communicate with her newborn, as well as the presence of my mother beside me to relieve me of this responsibility, and to give me from her motherhood wealth a knowledge that helps me to overcome this stage. Indeed, motherhood is not in the act of procreation and upbringing, but it is first a source of tenderness, and a stream of embracing. This is what I have been missing in my mother, who was preoccupied with prestige, and the fake joys of life made her forget the reality of motherhood and its sacrifices.

I was close to a fervent and passionate motherhood that cannot be flooded by all the seas of universe. I was a mother with my instinct, pain, loneliness, and torments, so I took Kamal from the first cuddle and tightened him to my chest, while he began to suckle tenderness with a great gluttony, as if his strangeness in my womb exceeded an eternity, as if he was thirsty to sip all this tenderness.

Mary, the nurse, stared at me and said:

- Madame ... I see in the glitter of your eyes the glow of motherhood, and I am sure that Kamal will be the happiest child with a mother like you.

Her words triggered the nostalgia in my depths and burned the tears that were still in my eyeballs, so I said to her:

- Mary, every mother sees her childhood in her children ... Kamal is the candle that illuminated the total darkness in my life.

The young nurse collected her stuff and went out muttering:

-   May God bless him and give him the most beautiful
    years...

I gathered my strength and broke the chains of my destructive emotions, for my journey began today with a child who came carrying hope and aspiration. Perhaps his presence between me and Adnan would ignite the flame of love, break the rigidity of domination, and make Adnan's heart kind toward us, so that he would feel love and forgive himself for what he did to me previously. I thought for a second that the crying of a baby would create an atmosphere of tenderness and cordiality in the halls of the house and would tighten the strings of the heart, so that the sun of prosperity and solidarity would shine on our lives ... I thought ...

The moment I entered the house carrying my child, all these assumptions and delusions fell ... The flames of fear and terror burned more than ever before, and the fangs of the housemaster appeared as a predatory beast, when he ordered me saying:

Stay at home and do not go beyond its threshold, for I am busy, and after my return we will talk about the rest...

The popular quote was true: "The mountain just gave birth to a mouse", as if I was a prisoner waiting for the date of her trial,and everything I dreamed of was dispersed in a second. I was afraid that having this cruelty would harm my baby, while he was not guilty of all that has happened and what will happen. I felt compelled to fight the confrontation war, since it was no longer permissible to compromise and humiliate, and my baby's right shall be one of the priorities. Therefore, I declared resistance between me and myself, and I thought about how to find a way to save my home from the fire of destruction, and to control the family very firmly, whatever the price and the huge sacrifices that would cost me.

Motherhood awakened Eve's savvy and love in my depths, so I gathered all the strengths to overcome the stormy torments in our marital life, and I sought wisdom and perspective to save my home from falling and collapsing. I shrewdly began showing love to Adnan, who was insistent on fending me off and forming estrangement between us for purposes almost unknown to me. I used to put the baby into his arms so that his heart become more compassionate, or let him watch me while I was breastfeeding him, hoping that his conditions would change, his heart softened, and all this coldness would dissipate. However, he remained in his sturdiness, and even increased the level of insults in order to fabricate disputes and to provoke conflicts and fights.

I was struggling with myself to endure his slut and tough behavior like a hard stone, as if I was living through a century of hardships. This is my fate and my destiny, while the image of my mother and the ugliness of her insistence on my marriage have become nightmares that chase me.

Today, I am reliving my childhood through my child who filled life with joy. I was straying in his innocent smile, feeling the pain upon his cry.

The black thoughts that usurped my happiness continued to chase me, and the questions eroded me... Is this woman who sold me when the first groom knocked on her door was in fact my mother?? Am I the daughter of a bastard who raised me and took care of me till the age of sixteen, then my existence bothered her, so she decided to leave me?? But how her heart obeyed that, when the cat preys on the street if anyone came near to her babies.

Is the motherhood they are talking about just nonsense? Never ... I became a mother, and my being was spiritually attached to my child, while every pulse of my heart prays for his peace.

Adnan's habit has changed, and he started to leave me and his baby at night without excuses, while I have no right to ask him about the reason of his absence. I started to pass nights alone, isolated within silent and cold walls. I began to feel this angel's fear for his mother without uttering it, as if he was hiding his suspicion behind looks scattered in the unknown. Blaming a bossy husband was extremely dangerous, whose results were severe beatings, physical and verbal violence, abuse, and recklessness, but I insisted on being courteous and polite, regardless of the results, to preserve the warmth of my home and keep my child away from the pain of separation in the future.

My task was very arduous for a wife who was imprisoned by cold emotions, neglect and torture, while Adnan's absence was repeated again and again, and the pace of quarrel was escalated day after day, until I felt as if I had entered hell with its scorching fire. My body was decorated with bruises of an unscrupulous monster, until one day Adnan disappeared. He left the house as if a ghost had crossed into my life by accident. He left me alone, without money or aid, while I was a weak and thin wife, with an innocent child in my arms in need of milk and medicine. I waited for his return for a long time, until I became suspicious and feared that he might be suffering something wrong. When the doors blocked in front of me, I carried my baby and went to the police station despite my horror, and reported my husband's absence despite my fear of his brutality. In addition to that, I was "bankrupt" without money, and my baby was hungry, so I entered, upon my return, a jewelry shop and sold a gold bracelet that Adnan had given me on our wedding day, hoping that it would fill one of my many needs. The world has become harder, and my day has become darker than my night, praying that he will come back quickly, and hoping that he might save me from a place in which I do not belong, as if a woman with no capability to manage her affairs, while having a child who was not yet one-year-old.

Months passed while I was imprisoned in a narrow spiral that even oxygen was lost in it, and where going out is forbidden unless absolutely necessary. After I reached a state of collapse, I decided to search for help and assistance by any person from my country, who would help me, support me, and pull me out of this deep well, since the police could not find Adnan or find a trace of him.

I picked up few things for my baby and wandered off the streets in scattered and unknown directions, while the heat devoured my steps with flames and burn.

Fate opposed me with its cruelty and oppression, and everything I did was pointless, until I caught by accident "Rose", who was absent from me. I felt psychologically a bit of moisture and refreshing, so I tracked down her steps trying to reach her, but the very high temperature of the baby deterred me from arrival, then Rose disappeared in the crowd, while I was filled with despair again, and I came home dead, bearing a soul groaning of sickness.

"There are times in life when you can feel the pain accumulated for long years" - Dostoevsky

---

I didn't cross the threshold of the house until I got a heavy smack, then slaps fell on my weak body and bruises surrounded me from all sides, to the point where the baby fell from my hands and I was unable to pick him up.I was screaming with all my energy, crying out, but there was no answer, so I lay down on my belly and crawled like a cat, while Adnan took the child to the bedroom, came back to drag me by my hair until the door of the house and throw me out without providing an excuse or a reason for his absence or a Fatwa to kick me out, and he started repeating one phrase:

- Get out ... get out of the house ... I can't imagine your presence here.

How could I go and my soul in the bedroom? How do I go while my baby is imprisoned in his dark prison? I begged himand kissed his feet while he was not concerned about the suffering of a mother, promising that he would not give me the baby except after the divorce. My heart almost stopped beating, my breath slowly suffocated in my chest and my face began to deluge with tears, so I begged him to divorce me and to have mercy and give me my baby.

32

Adnan played the game of tyrants, so he bargained with me for the dowry, and demanded five million pounds to break my imprisonment and to release me from his chains.

He was a monster covered by the clothes of Adam, a human being that lacks conscience, compassion and humanity, a sick, worn out, rotten spirit, and a satanic soul.

I spent my night as a wounded animal perched at the house door, while he was falling into a deep sleep. I started eavesdropping to check on my baby, since I was afraid of harming him, so the idea of seeking help from the Police came to me, in order to return my baby.

At the crack of dawn, I caught my pain and ran to the nearest police station to rush to the rescue. But when we entered the house, Adnan had disappeared with the baby, so I melted down and fell unconscious. I waited for a long time at the threshold of the house, hoping he would come back, but my wait was long and the world began to go black in my eyes. I was lost in a tumultuous storm of thoughts.

His disappearance lasted for days, and I was still waiting at the door of the house in which Rose lived after she became his master, where I was the servile one who was thrown outside. I remained rigid and stiff and I was not strong enough to move, and I could not even break free from the state of silence. I was as if a wedge nailed in the frame of a painful painting drenched in a depth of sorrows, except for my tears, which refused but to sprout out of my eyes. Only a drop remained until I've had enough, and I would die from sadness for what happened to me. Even Rose, her heart was broken to what my condition turned out to be, so she was throwing me a few bites of her food, asking me after a long time to enter the house only in case I wanted to pee and to change my clothes. As if she was telling me to keep my stubbornness, but in vain, until Adnan appeared again. At that time, my milk had dried up, so I begged him to give me my son, my baby, my soul, but he insisted on the bargaining deal in return for giving up my child and my divorce paper.

How can I bring five million pounds for him when I don't have the money for food? How?? He prevented me from waiting even in front of the house, saying: I want to stay there with my wife.

- What?? Your wife??

His last phrase fell like a knife in my flank, like someone flogging my dignity and my self-esteem, so I asked him in a suffocated voice:

- Are you married Adnan?

He answered me coldly:

- Yes, I am married and Rose is my wife, and I was subject to my family's decision when I married you, but I realized that I cannot live without her, it is my whole life ... Come on, get out of here.

How easy it is for you to leave! How do I leave without the baby, how do I leave my own child in the hands of a stepmother?

He threw his mold body on the sofa and went on to say:

- So waive your right, bring the sum, take your baby, and go away from me ... I have no other words.

"I wish there were two copies of me so I could pat my back".
– Paul Oster

I picked up my wounds after he kicked me out and forcibly closed the door behind me. I sat hysterically slapping my face, but at least I discovered a truth that was a mystery to me, and I realized that he had married me to forget a stormy love in his heart.

I was the victim of a fraud and deceitful marriage that an innocent soul who is our baby paid the price thereof. I discovered a mystery as if I was watching a drama that was so touching and even destructive.

I began to moan intermittently. I raised my hands to above seeking the relief of God, and I decided to face the storm. I will not let this trouble break me or destroy my resolve, for a weak person can suffer the trouble twice if he was helpless, and it shall spread through his being, as cancer spreads in the body.

A devastated woman, deprived of her baby, wandering like a raging bull, spinning in a vicious circle, while her depths are loaded with oppression, injustice and hunger. He kicked me out of the house as a dead body without a soul. I had passed through the crowds of streets and alleys among pedestrians, where I saw the faces as nothing but idols in front of me, and I started to derive my strength from my weakness. It was necessary to find shelter and work in order to be able to face and confront. I was eavesdropping in public hoping to find someone who spoke my language and whose color was close to the color of my skin, until I came across an elegant lady, in whom oriental features were found, arguing with a fabric seller about the price. I approached her with great fear saying:

- Good evening.

She looked at me with a fleeting glance, but then she stared at me with my shabby clothes and my bad shape saying:

- Are you Lebanese? Good evening.

I answered her in a trembling voice:

- Yeah.

- You live in the country? She said it very cautiously.

I answered timidly:

- Yeah.

She calmed down, so she continued:

- Hurray ... I am.....

38

I interrupted her before introducing herself to me in a voice of hope:

- Madame, do you want a maid in your house?

I uttered these words with tears on my cheeks, and while pain was squeezing my heart and hunger was squeezing my intestines.

I was astonished by myself and decided to cut the conversation off, then she went away without continuing her words. However, I extended my bruised hand and tried to stop her, but she continued her walk, not caring about my situation as if she was afraid of me, so I followed her like a dog follows his owner step by step.

Every second she turned back to watch me following her footsteps, wondered by my foolish act. For me, she was a glimmer of hope in the darkness that surrounds my life, so I begged and entreated her to accept me as a servant in her house, until she was unable to handle me more, so she screamed at me in anger:

- Won't you stop chasing me?

Then she threatened me to send the janitor to kick me out if I continued chasing her. I returned to the street, shedding a lot of tears, with a great heartbreak, humiliation and insult.

She stood behind the window watching me, as I slept on the sidewalk like beggars, wandering, lost and homeless. She felt sympathy for me, so she came to my side and asked me with a pity smile:

-       There is no place for you to go?

Her question warmed my heart, refreshed my being and bloomed my dead senses, as if I had touched a faint glimmer of light, so I replied:

-       No!

With this answer, I summarized my suffering, my tragedy and my baby loss, so she gave me her hand to be able to get up, and said:

-       I see you exhausted and devastated by hunger. Don't you want food?

A smile appeared on my lips after it has been absent since my arrival to Africa, and I said to her:

-       I will do whatever work you want from me.

She looked at me this time with kindness, and said:

-       You are very thin, pale, and tired.

I nodded my head affirmatively.

She walked in front of me, then turned to me, saying:

-       Follow me.

I stopped her for a moment and told her:

-       Madame, I will do whatever work you shall ask for, I will not consider it pity or charity, for I am a victim of force majeure that compelled me to be the way I am.

She tied her long hair with a scrunchie, and I walked with her like a driven sheep. I felt a little safe when I entered the house, while she hurried to serve me food, and asked me to rest a little. Her features and behavior have changed towards me, and my heart started to recover, then she came with cleaning tools and guided me to the kitchen and the bathrooms.

Her kitchen was clean, and so were the bathrooms, yet she asked me to clean. I started to succeed in my new mission like a bull breaks through the wastelands, as she headed to the living room to watch a TV series she was apparently following.

When I finished cleaning, I came to her, and she gave me a financial reward. She didn't talk to me, but rather told me to leave. I felt heartbroken, with a great loss in my pride, but I clung to the question and asked her:

-       Don't you want me to come back again?

She nodded her head yes, accompanied by a smile of satisfaction. My heart danced with joy, and I raced with its beats as a bird released from its prison cage, without thinking of where I would spend my night.

I no longer care about the outdoors, nor the woe of homelessness on the sidewalks of a country where everything is strange, and the exile is no longer my obsession and my fears. All that mattered to me was embracing my child, getting him back and returning life to my soul, for I am ready to tear and crucify my body on the tree of sacrifice for the sake of my angel.

I entered the street across her house, fearing that I would miss the address again, and waited for the nightfall, where I returned like a thief to the house yard, and extended my tired body over the garden grass, succumbing to a deep sleep. However, someone felt my presence and approached me frightened at first, then woke me up wondering:

-      Who are you? How did you get here?

He was Lebanese, gorgeous, broad-shouldered, of moderate stature, in the middle of his fourth decade of age. I begged him, pleading to protect myself, and I told him the secret of my stay in this lonely place, and that the owner of the house asked me to

42

return again, so I was afraid that I would miss the address and decided to stay here.

I touched compassion in his eyes. He barely turned his back to leave me alone until the lady of the house stood in front of me, astonished at why I was there. He informed her about the conversation between us, as if she realized that I was homeless, while this man asked me to enter the house and sleep in a narrow room that seemed to be a room for servants.

The time had passed one o'clock in the morning, and there was no way to continue the conversation, so the master of the house entered, while the lady led me to the intended room.

I noticed that a dispute took place between the spouses, and I realized that there was no way to stay in this house tomorrow, thereafter sleepiness flew off my eyelids, and black thoughts chased me, so I became afraid again to return to the street.

As soon as the morning sends its first light, I surreptitiously stepped out of the house and waited like a beggar at the door, hoping that this family again will have sympathy towards my condition, and that mercy enlighten their hearts.

Its daylight and the street began to be crowded, while I remained peeping until the master of the house went out to work. As soon as he got out and turned his engine, I knocked on the door and I was sure that the lady would kick me out hardly.

She opened the door, surprised by what happened last night, and in her looks many question marks, so I realized the matter and preceded her, saying:

Yesterday, I didn't want to cause any inconvenience, so I went out at dawn and waited outside.

She stared in the space as if she was secretly praying to God, then she invited me to re-enter and made me a delicious breakfast. This morning, she was a different woman, who had features radiating kindness and compassion.

After breakfast, she brought a coffee pot and sat in front of me after she offered me a cup, while she started to interrogate with me:

-       What is your story, woman? You look like a young polite flower-girl? What happened to you in Abidjan? What is your secret?

A question which refreshed my entity. I finally felt that there is someone who can hear me and listen to my tragedy. I began to tell her my story or my journey with torment, and I noticed tears in her eyes and eagerness in her face, especially when I told her with great heartache about my son, my baby and his unknown fate. She sympathized with me as if she knew me before, and whispered, saying:

-    You will help me today, and I will talk to one of my friends about you, since she is a working woman and is looking for a non-African housekeeper to take care of her children, thus securing you a good accommodation and a pleasant livelihood.

I could not hold my feelings, so I bowed and kissed her hands, while she raised me from the ground, saying:

-    Girls who have been raised well are created to be honored, not to be insulted.

I spent this day different from all the days I have lived since coming to this country. I felt safe, kind, and psychologically comfortable, while she called her husband, informed him of my circumstances, and begged him to accept my survival, until she secured me a decent job to earn a living from.

In the evening, I prepared the dinner table and went back to the kitchen thinking alone with an eagerness to cuddle my baby. After dinner, I did all my duties, then I lay down on the floor in the servant's little room, and fell asleep calmly and deeply. I recalled my childhood while wandering my toys like a butterfly strolling in flower fields, when I had a room and a roof that protected me from the treachery of time, so I missed my grandfather's embrace of safety, his fairy tales, and his southern heroics during the French occupation of my homeland. I miss my swing hanging in the old oak tree in front of our home in the village. The return of memories, and my grandfather's face pulled me out of the gap of sadness and humiliation, so I fell asleep until the golden rays of the sun tickled my eyelids, and I realized that my day had begun again and there was something awaiting me in the unknown. However, a terrible pain crippled me from trying, as if my steps were paralyzed, but I struggled and hastened to prepare the breakfast before the family woke up.

I touched an indescribable pleasure in the eyes of Mrs. Reem, and I knew her name this morning when her husband called her. They had breakfast and she bid him farewell, then she entered the kitchen and found me washing the dishes. She turned off the water tap and said:

-       Come.

-       What?

- Come on, I'll give you some clothes of mine. You look close to my size, but first go to the bathroom and take a shower.

- But?

- Don't argue with me. Come on hurry up, since we will make a visit.

I entered the bathroom a fragile, humiliated person, not like women, and I came out another woman whose features still have some femininity and charm. She gifted me a floral dress, flat shoes and a little bit of fragrance, and we went out together.

The distance of the trip was very short, and the conversation was almost short between us, while her gaze contained a lot of mercy and compassion. It was only minutes before we reached a high-rise building, which contains many apartments, so we took the elevator to the third floor, and Mrs. Reem rang the bell. A baby girl looks like an angel opened the door and immediately reminded me of my baby who was far from me, then she said to her mother:

- My aunt Reem ... my aunt Reem ...

The apartment looked elegant, exquisitely decorated, spacious salon, and on either side of the long corridor there were some

47

rooms. One of the balconies was decorated with luxurious "Mahogany" wood and a large crystal chandelier shone with glow, while the walls were decorated with nature drawings and luxurious oil paintings.

Everything in this home expresses high-taste, luxury and sophistication.

Suddenly, the owner of the house came with a charm and a captivating presence, her luxurious clothes reflect a high class, adorned with jewelry, and she warmly welcomed her guest.

I sat next to Mrs. Reem, afraid to raise my eyes to the owner of the house. The conversation between them was full of mysteries and haze until Mrs. Reem asked me to enter the kitchen to make coffee for them. The owner of the house guided me to her kitchen, which at first glance seemed to be a masterpiece, and placed in my hands coffee, sugar and cups, then returned to her guest.

I returned with a coffee pot and cups on the tray, and the gazes of the house owner were sharp and frightening. She took the tray and ordered me to go back to the kitchen to complete her conversation with Mrs. Reem ... I waited long and my fears intensified, but something in my heart was reassuring, then I heard Mrs. Reem's voice calling me. I hastened like a wind, perhaps she wanted to leave, and I almost stood in front of them until she said:

Um Kamal, you will stay with Mrs. Hind, reside with her and supervise her housekeeping. You will be safe, Um Kamal.

I couldn't gather my words, and I only found myself hugging her with intense gratitude. The phrase "Um Kamal" was a tone that seeped into the depths of my heart and cut off its veins.

Mrs. Reem tightened my hand and continued:

-    I really trust you.

She left me with a heart touching goodbye, after she ordered the house owner, Hind, to take care of me, then she left.

"This life will not stop to take into account your sadness ... Either you will stand and complete it despite your brokenness ... or you will remain forever lying." -Che Guevara

I finally began a new stage of my struggle and research to discover the unknown.

I started a step different from my previous ones, and I was not bothered by all things except one thing, is how to take back my child in order to feel that my entity and soul returned to me.

Hind seemed to be serious and too firm. Her features were harsh, with a bit of arrogance, and she was in her third decade of life. She was of a medium height and had a short curly hair. She guided me to the place where I should sleep on the floor in the kitchen, and she started dictating to me her orders and informing me about her house order. She was well versed in treating servants cruel and mercilessly, so there was no way for wasting time with her, since she considered that every second was useful for something and that work shall be from dawn till the end of the night.

My day began when Mrs. Reem left, while she came to me with a lot of tasks such as washing dishes, sweeping the house, then polishing the glass and taking care of the children. Little by little I began to get used to my tasks.

She surrounded me with her orders, and I was shocked by the low salary that she had allocated to me. She fabricated arguments to always complain about work time and to make me feel wrong, and she used to shout and get angry at me, especially after Mrs. Reem sent me the clothes, as she insisted that I wear the servants' clothes and that I remain prisoned in the kitchen.

Time passed while I was at her service. I never heard from her except complaints and grumblings, and whenever Mrs. Reem visited her, she fabricated lies and delusions, but Mrs. Reem understood her intentions and always whispered to me:

- Eating to live is difficult, and my house is small, so I cannot employ anyone; be patient with your situation until we find a solution to your case.

I felt an indescribable tenderness from Mrs. Reem, a kind heart that was hidden behind a cloud of severity, and a big heart full of compassion and benevolence; therefore, I was patient with the behavior and tyranny of "Hind", while receiving all kinds of contempt and insult and enduring her oppression to secure the money for that predator, in order to take back my child.

The most painful thing for me was my heart which bled with all forms of longing for being away from my son who dug grooves between the folds of my soul, and poured out a flood of tears as I yawned every evening. A long time has passed, but I had to put my feelings out of my days. in which my thirst for Kamal does not quench except for the magic of his eyes that resides inside my soul. I was aware every time and every moment that we would meet one day, walk on open paths together, and turn our dreams into reality.

I will resist and defeat fate to take back my son and to fill him again with my love.

One day I noticed an unusual movement in the house, and travel bags filled all over the living room with the noise of children jogging, where the three were positioned on the door shouting:

-    Papa has arrived ... Papa has arrived.

I immediately realized that the house owner was coming, returning from a travel trip, so I stayed in my place. When he entered the house, Hind called me, and I saw in front of me a man in his mid-forties, tall, with a huge body and big eyes, bald; and as if I saw another wife, opposite of what I knew, reeling and coquetting, sometimes throwing into his arms and sometimes embracing him.

I got confused, and imagined how Adnan was dealing with cruelty and persecution. The master of the house was astonished at my presence, and his eyes were clearly confused, so Hind avoided the situation, saying:

-      This is Elham my beloved Nasser ... the new maid.

Her words fell like a whip on my soul, and I felt an unlimited insult, as if she intended to introduce me in this hurtful way, and she did not replace the word "maid" with the new "housekeeper". She treated me as if I were a slave, while I was the girl who grew up in a simple family, I am the bride who did not complete her first year of marriage, the bride that was betrayed by her husband who kidnapped her baby from her, and urged her to work as a maid in an unknown house and with a catty and bullying woman ...

Servants for some rascal people are just servants, scum in their point of view, but the husband showed more tenderness than she did, so he smiled, saying:

-      Hey ... are you Lebanese?

I nodded my head yes, then turned to the corner that the house owner had dedicated for me: the kitchen.

I noticed something urgent, and I felt suspicious and worried about the looks of Mr. Nasser that chased me. I wondered if he was the type of philanderer men, striving after their desires, is it possible for a well-to-do businessman to like a poor and helpless maid.

I used to spend the nights awake, while my loneliness suffers from nostalgia for cuddling my baby, and a great heartburn for touching him, and I wonder how he is now? How does he live? How does Rose take care of him? These questions were increasing the pain of my soul. I pretended to be asleep for fear, and listened to Mrs. Hind's footsteps as she peeked to see if I was asleep or still awake. I realized what was going through her mind and what she suffers from.

This night was completely different from previous nights. The footsteps of the wanderer in the house were light, almost as if they were the steps of a thief trying to steal. I pretended to be in a deep sleep, but a cold hand rested on my shoulder, and a whispering voice called me almost like a susurrus.

- Elham!

I opened my eyes to see Mr. Nasser leaving his marital bed and visiting me in the darkness, a visit that was full of desire, and in the sparkle of his eyes there was a glint of lust and a wild desire. He whispered again and said:

- Elham!

I sat frightened and answered him:

- Yeah.

He continued saying:

-        Obey me and you will gain much, for you are a young woman, full of life, who needs someone to take care of her, embrace her, and cuddle her with his love.

Frankly, at first I did not understand his words and his intent, so I felt a shiver shaking my being. I looked at him with fierce looks filled with fear, while he patted my shoulder saying:

-        Go to sleep and do not be afraid... I am the angel sent by the Creator to protect you and provide you with safety... Sleep, Elham.

Then he went back to the bedroom, hidden by the night dark, while I was confined to myself, realizing that there was no place for me in this house after this night, and what the unknown holds for me is more painful than what I have experienced, as I will not be able to save the money to get my baby back. I felt in his looks unconditional lust to prey me, and what I feared has happened... What would my fate be if I refused to respond to him?

Returning to the street... But how will Mrs. Reem believe that I am maltreated...Oh my God! Why all this torment, this oppression and humiliation? I have no choice but to escape before disaster strikes and the fire breaks out...

Only to escape...

The dawn broke, awaken in its silence and awe. I packed my things and intended to leave with a horrible, devastating feeling, and a terror which swept through my being, believing that the sustenance came from the Lord of the worlds. I endured all this humiliation to save the sum that my unscrupulous husband demanded, to get my baby back, and since I had saved some money to rent a room which shall include my tragedies while I could find another job. All the fear I had if I was unable to protect myself and that this despicable man will prey on my flesh and defile my honor. When the sun rose, I entered the living-room where Mrs. Hind was sipping her morning coffee and I stood in front of her. She was surprised by my act and stared at me with angry looks, then I told her:

-        I want to leave.

She did not understand the sentence at first, but astonishment fell on her face and she took a few seconds to grasp my words, then said:

-        Why?

My audacity in revealing the truth and what her vile husband had tried to do betrayed me, and confusion was evident on my features, so I tried to search for arguments, until I told her:

-       I got tired of working and my health is no longer helping me to continue, so I was afraid that I would fall short in my work, and my back pain increased a lot, even painkillers no longer work.

The cruelty faded away from her features and said:

-       Well, rest today and divide your work tasks, the children and I got used to you.

I seized the opportunity of her sudden change of condition, and I told her: Work has exhausted me.

She replied:

-       Do you want me to give you a whole day off every week? Then she took two steps closer and stared at me with hope, then said:

-       Listen to me Elham, I am aware that I have tired you lately and have been hard on you, and I am aware of the trouble you are suffering and enduring. What do you think if we visit the doctor, as he is a friend of the family, to examine you and check on your health?

Her words made me happy and her offer seduced me, so I responded saying:

-       But, Mrs. Hind…

She interrupted me with a satisfied smile:

- I will reduce your work responsibilities, and allocate a schedule for each day, for the children got accustomed to you and to your tenderness, and I am relieved of your presence.

I whispered to myself: It will be my weekly day off to see my baby even from afar, for my heart is on fire, but will Hind be satisfied to leave the house? I hesitated a lot to accept the offer since my courage betrayed me, but the cry of my baby, which does not leave my memory, urged me to take action. So, I proposed to her what was on my mind about my child while I was waiting for a refusal.

Silent moments prevailed between us... Each of us meditated on the other, as if we were evaluating each other. Then she nodded to me saying:

- Well, you shall have what you desire, and this day will be the Sunday of every week you leave to visit your baby, spend a long time with him and return in the evening before six p.m.

I felt a sigh of joy and happiness and my tears poured out of my eyes. I secretly asked: My God, what changed her attitude suddenly, and how the cruelty in her heart turned into tenderness, when she would go crazy if she saw me standing on the balcony? I am trying to escape from a fate that is chasing after me and blocking the openings in front of me. Her response confused me, so I told her:

- But Madame…

She gently patted my shoulder, interrupting, and said:

- Come on... Come on, go into the kitchen and put your things back in order, and next Sunday is your first day off.

My first day off… Oh my God, how wide is your generosity! I am your weak slave who groans from the pain of deprivation to embrace her infant, and dreams for a moment to regain her stolen freedom. How can I sleep when my eyelids refuse to surrender? Will this day be my space where I feel free? Why not, when on that day I will carry a gift for my baby, cuddle him, dry the sweat from his forehead, and be a shadow hovering over him until I can secure the ransom to bring him back...?

Hours and moments passed quickly as if a passing tape, and my feelings blazed like firewood in the hearth of tenderness. The awaited Sunday came after a long nostalgia. I woke up before dawn and prepared myself to go out, and when the eight o'clock struck, I was waiting for a taxi to take me to my baby's house, but I remembered the toy, so I roamed the streets to choose a toy for a child who is not interested in toys as much as he misses his mother's embrace. The world of children is very beautiful, and all the toys therein are the same, but musical games have a special taste since they tickle his senses and draw laughter on his mouth... I searched for a long time until I bought him a train that emits lights and music, and waited in front of his house entrance. I waited so long that the heat of the afternoon almost hit my head, and the flames of the sun burn my body like the venom of a spotted snake.

Why don't you dare knock on the door? Your child Kamal is waiting for you... I gathered my strength and knocked on the latch of the house once... twice... thrice... The door opened and Rose stood right in front of me... In front of my house door in which I gave my life to a rapist husband, this place which is supposed to be my refuge and the source of my happiness.

As soon as Rose mumbled words that I did not understand due to my complete mind-wandering, so that words were lost from me and my tongue only uttered the name of Kamal, until Adnan appeared with his mischievous face and angry features. Glory be to God, as if I saw him for the first time. He was deformed, and the features of hate appeared on his face.

He got shocked by my presence where anger lurked in his eyes, then he screamed loudly as if a wailing jackal lost his prey, saying:

-        What do you want?! What brings you here...?

While he was completely furious about my visit, I saw Kamal crawling and moving with his first steps, as if he was expressing with his eyes:

-        Mom... I miss your cuddle...

I felt as if I had owned the world and everything therein, and I hurried to cuddle him to my chest, to my inner soul, but Adnan was faster than my longing, so he pulled me away from him and roared at me like a predator, saying:

-        Go away... I can't handle seeing you in my house... You mean nothing to me.

I took the encouragement as a predatory cat, and revealed my claws in front of him, saying:

-        This is my son, and no power will stop me from seeing him. Do you understand what I'm saying?
He said:

-        Forget about this baby. He is no longer your son. Leave us, you have nothing to do with this family… Leave us in peace.
I started to beg him, and Kamal was bursting into tears, while Rose was watching what was going on, as if she had achieved a round of a victory battle and defeated me hardly after taking control of Adnan and cancelling his personality.

Is it possible that this man who married me was so blind and insightful in order to have sex with this kind of woman?

I imagined myself as the ghost of a defeated woman, striving to retrieve her baby.

I took a deep breath and said:

-    Let me give this toy to Kamal... Let me feel my motherhood...

He pushed me out, pounced on the toy like a predator, and threw it harshly to the ground as if he was breaking my heart into pieces, then shouted at me:

-    Get out of my face and don't come back until you have five million with you. After that you can claim that you have a baby.

He closed his door in my face, as if I were a beggar, and I came to ask for money. Where is the justice of the sky?! Where is mercy in the hearts?! I wish I had died before I could be sure with my own eyes and see this insult and this humiliation.

Naji I.b

> "when you get through a difficult phase in your life, continue life as a survivor not as a victim" - Jalaluddin Rumi

The idea of death was my only escape and my lifeline from this abuse. Adnan looked like a dog barking over a corpse in the presence of his masters...

A vile man, in which nastiness creeps into himself.

I healed the wounds of mine with disappointment and went back to Hind's house, perhaps I could recover my solace among her children, warming my heart with the shadow of their laughter, until I settle the value of the ransom, and retrieve my child from this man's hell.

My feet were weary like an ill struggling with life, while Hind greeted me with shock, surprise and pity, then she hurried and brought a cup of cold water and started patting my shoulder. When I regained my breath, I told her the truth of what had happened... She shivered with clear sparks of anger in her eyes, and said:

-    May God's curse be upon him...a person without mercy or conscience; he does not fear God.

Hind calmed me down; Then I entered the kitchen to collect the remains of my baby's toy, as if I were collecting parts of my broken heart, wounded by the deep pain of a mother who was deprived from her child by oppression. I became despaired and realized that my battle was bitter and fate was standing against my way.

I slept on my pillow with fear, and the face of Kamal never left me, a baby like an angel in the stories pious lives; He seemed young in his first steps and a man in his raped childhood.

I decided to provide the ransom to get both of him and my freedom.

I am a woman of weak strength, but tough; No matter how painful the executioner's whips are, the mercy of heaven must be awaited...I must abandon my heart for a while, forget it, suppress my emotions, and plan cleverly as Eve to recover my usurped rights; for life is like a crutch to lean on, if it breaks, we fall into a deep abyss from which it is difficult for us to get out...From now on it will be my job to provide the ransom to humiliate this usurper and throw the money in his face.

From this moment on, I am another woman, rebellious, revolutionary, and as a lighthouse that will eventually dock at the shore of revenge. Here I am, with my remaining strength, declaring my rebellion against life to reach what I want, and soon, God willing...I will sleep, but my longing for Kamal will remain awake, for he is the absent hope, awakening in my inner soul and future. Life, with all its stages and circumstances, will not be able to break me, and my pain will be tomorrow a mirror that reflects my strength and my joys, since weakness only makes us broken and depressed.

This morning, I was leaning towards my heart when the sun's rays were sewing a golden shawl for me. I smelled the breeze of freedom that spread its vibes around my weary body, and it started stealing from my life for moments and days. Soon we will meet, my dear and my life soul, and I will embrace you as clouds roll over the moon, for you are my obsession...I woke up unusually active and started my housework, waiting for the children to come back from school, and after lunch I made sure to give them a shower. In the evening, I prepared the table for the couple, trying to avoid approaching Mr. Nasser, then I returned to my solitude and to the dark painful nights alone with my thoughts.

This night was different from the rest of the nights. It was quiet, calm, and I convinced myself that what Mr. Nasser had done was a moment of enthusiasm. However, my thoughts deceived me and my certainty betrayed me, since he slinked and lay near me while his wife was out of the house staying with her sister who had given birth to her first child. I rose up like a slaughtered bird dancing in pain, and I felt as if my soul had left my body, so I hurried to the hall, but he followed me, trying to mute my voice, and he encircled me in his arms as a prisoner is chained in captivity.

I fled quickly out of his arms into the kitchen, losing focus. I placed the knife in his face, while he went steps back and said in a trembling voice:

-      Crazy girl, take it easy, I only want to help you. Your situation is difficult.

Then he wiped the sweat from his forehead and said:

-      My tenderness will give you strength and security.

I kept my balance with the knife in my hand, and said to him:

-      I do not want anything from you ...

He looked at me with cunning, malice and brutality, and said:

-      Well, tomorrow morning you leave the house before Madame comes back...

He went back to his room to be indulged in the mud of his animal instinct, while I was shivering.

It's my last day in this house... Tomorrow morning, I will return to the street and my dream of meeting my child returns to a mirage, so that I became homeless with my mental pain and anguish. I couldn't sleep, and I sat with the knife in my hand, waiting for the dawn to come. My night was long with dark thoughts and frightful nightmares. As soon as the morning shone, I gathered a bundle of my remains and wandered in the streets like clockwork, but my feeling led me unwillingly to Mrs. Reem's house, so I hurried to knock on the door. She was astonished when she saw me in my condition, and said:

-        Elham, what are you doing here at this hour?

She accompanied me to the living- room, then began to calm me, while my tears were pouring down on my cheeks, and my breath choked. After this crying, I regained some of my energy, and started telling her my story, and my heart was almost out òf my chest.

At first, she doubted my words, and I noticed this through her looks, then she said:

-        Unbelievable! What do you say!? Mr. Nasser is a wise, sober and respectful man, who loves his wife and is devoted to her service.

I told her:

- That's what happened, Mrs. Reem.

With a capable touch, she felt the sincerity of my words, so she rose from her place and said:

-        Well, don't say a word; This is a disaster that may destroy a home and make a family homeless!! The problem is what are you going to do now! I cannot host you in my narrow house.

I wiped my tears with my sleeve and told her:

- God is generous, I will look for a modest room, knowing that I am fully aware of my return to the street, and I will strive to find a job for my livelihood.

"I will not regret anyone who entered my life and left, the faithful made me happy, the bad gave me the experience, the worst was a lesson for me, the best would never leave me." - Mahatma Gandhi

---

I left with a broken heart, for the people who are safe in their homes do not care about the homelessness of the weak and the poor people...I lay on the bed the first night, waiting for the mercy of heaven. The next day, I went looking for an honorable livelihood, and found accommodation with a family who had a room for rent. I rented it and packed my things therein after I had paid a rental for two months in advance, then I brought a pillow and a mattress, and obtained liberty that was in their hands.

I returned again the next day to look for a work... I kept knocking on the doors but in vain, and in the evening I was going back to my room with a dead body and some breath. This situation remained for long days, and no one would give trust to a white woman in Africa to work in his house as a maid, to the extent that I almost lost hope and got despair. While I was daily homeless at God's door, searching for work under the sun's heat that stung my skinny body, I met by chance Mrs. Hind who stopped me asking: What did you do? Is this what we deserve from you? How could you betray the trust? I told her:

-       Which trust?

She said nervously:

-        Are you ignoring it? You stole my husband's wallet and you ran away. What do you call your behavior? Is this the promise that I entrusted to you in my absence?

I felt as if she twisted a knife in my heart until the core, and in a stifled voice and a deep heartburn, I replied:

-        But, Madame…

She shouted at me with anger:

-        Perhaps what happened to you in your life is because of what you were doing.

I told her:

-        You are wronging me, Madame.

She said excitedly angry:

-        Don't interrupt me.

I was weak and cowardly at that moment, and I could not defend myself since she simply did not hurt me during my stay in her house, but later bestowed upon me all the sympathy; If I told her the truth, I would destroy her.I hid what happened in my heart, maintained my dignity and her family, and consented to be unjust to myself but not revealing a bitter truth that might ruin a home.

I returned back, and instead of going to my petty room, I went to Mrs. Reem's house and told her what had happened with me, she said:

\-   God bless you, Elham, since you did not tell her about what happened, and I believe your words, but there is no power or strength save in God. The poor must always pay the price and bears the mistakes of the rich at the expense of his dignity. You and your work are a victim, but the Lord of the worlds is with the patient and he will reward you with the best due to your good deed and provide you with a generous sustenance. You are a good-hearted and genuine woman who does not deserve this bitterness.

I begged her to strive for revealing my innocence one day in front of Hind, since the oppressed, even if days go by, his innocence revives him, so she nodded her head and said:

\-   Don't worry, for injustice is a crime and your innocence must one day reveal.

I felt very isolated in my room, as if I were in a tomb; so I began to go out every day to search for a work. Today, while I was wandering the streets, a man in his thirties stopped me and asked:

-    Do you speak Arabic? I told him:

-    Yeah.

He said:

-    Do you know where I can find a pharmacy?

Without hesitation, I asked him:

-    Do you know if anyone wants a maid?

He marveled at my discursive question in response to his question, and said:

-    I need a pharmacy right now.

I had memorized the shops and sidewalks, and even the faces due to my frequent walks and wanderings, so I said:

-    Yeah. There, on the corner of the street.

Seriously and earnestly replied:

-    Okay! Accompany me.

I wondered and said:

-    To where?

-    Come with me and then I shall ask my mother if she wants someone to take care of her in the house, for she is an old woman who lives alone and refuses to move to live with my family since my father's death, as she does not want to be a burden to anyone and that her presence will disturb the comfort of my family.

I looked at the sky and thanked God, then said to him:

-       Okay!

I walked behind him like a shadow chasing after his own, and my steps were dancing with joy.

Perhaps happiness will come through this coincidence! Why not?!

Coincidence has changed a lot of our lives' paths... I waited for him outside when he entered the pharmacy, but he was only seconds late until I followed him like a child afraid of being lost.

He was walking beside the street where Adnan lived. My heart began to tremble and I was afraid that I would miss the opportunity, but he continued until he stopped in front of a building, short distance away from the building in which my son lives. Oh my God, there's a crossroad distance between me and my child, so that I can peek at him! I prayed with a broken heart to have this opportunity.

My companion knocked on the door two times until an elderly woman, with a smile on her lips and a clear faith in her features, opened the door and surprised that I was with her son, so she asked:

-       Why did you come at this unusual hour, my son? You are supposed to be at home with your family.

She sighed with the tenderness of a mother, and said:

-       Are you hungry?

Then she turned, pointing her questioning gaze to me. Who is this girl? My companion embraced her in his arms and said:

-       With your consent, and for the last time, I ask you without despair to come with me to my house.

The good old woman patted his shoulder and said to him:

-       Son, this matter for me has been over for a long time, I only rest in my house with my memories and nostalgia for your absent father, I live here with your childhood.

He turned to me and then turned to her asking:

-       Well, my last hope, why don't you let this girl stay with you and help you? God knows better, but she looks of good manner and is looking for a job.

The old woman looked at me gently, and said to him:

-       Do you know her before?

I interrupted the dialogue with hope, as if God helped me to speak, so I said to her:

-       Try me, Madame, and if I bother you, dismiss me at once. Even if I cannot stay with you, I can come every day to tidy up the house and help you, then I will leave in the evening.

76

The old woman sensed the injustice of my condition and became emotional, while I continued to speak, and said to her:

- I urgently need any work.

She stared at me by the experience of her long life and her heart was filled with sympathy, then said:

- Fine, come tomorrow, and goodness is in what God has chosen, but you are young, so do you have experience in managing household affairs?

I answered quickly:

- More than you can imagine.

She gave me a look of tenderness, and said:

- Leave now and come back tomorrow, so that I can prepare a place for you to stay.

I left and a feeling of joy obsessed me... Life is almost smiling at me, shining a glimpse of hope in my darkness, bringing me closer to my child whom I am deprived of seeing, touching and embracing him.

I went back to my deserted room, which was for cold days without dreams, to reduce my wakefulness and fall into a short sleep for fear of being late to the old woman in the morning. I was sometimes asleep and sometimes awake, so at last I preferred to sit and wait for the morning. Is there a more beautiful and kind morning than the coming one? I packed my things and clothes and handed over the room key to the owners, although I did not get my money back, which I had paid for two months in advance, and hurriedly ran to the house of the kind old woman that God gave me, as a blessing, a mercy and a compassion.

My steps were faster than the wind, and my face refused to look but only at the building where my baby was. I knocked on the door and waited for the old woman to open it, knowing that I was afraid that she would change her mind or that she might have Alzheimer's disease...After a long wait, she opened the door as if it was a door of heaven for me and hugged me gently, so I told her:

-    Ask me and wish, and be sure that your orders will be executed.

She was amazed at my frankness and seemed astonished, but I went on:

-    You are the power of my happiness that opened in front of me, and I will be your obedient servant as long as I live, Madame.

She embraced me again, and I felt the tenderness of motherhood while I was in her hug. She said:

-    We, my daughter, are the servants of God, and no person has a command on anybody. We have been freed from slavery and ignorance, and we are the masters of ourselves and the children of God. We were created equal and free. Come on, let me show you your room.

My room was modest, with a window overlooking the street, and a small balcony overlooking the house from which I was expelled and where my baby is still confined... I was pleased with this balcony, which I considered my only refuge, and I sighed from the bottom of my heart with closed eyes, is it a dream or a reality?! Until the old woman's voice woke me up from my distraction, saying:

- What is your name, my daughter?

- You can't imagine, O master of grace, how much "my daughter's word" made me happy! I repeated it secretly, then replied:

- Elham.

She took two steps towards me, then said:

- Come on, Elham, and pack whatever you think needs to be organized, and let's prepare the food... After today, we must stick to a regular time when we eat our food, since having two on the table works up an appetite.

From the moment I came to this house, I began to organize work and schedule tasks, especially since the house is inhabited by an elderly woman who lives with her memories. Everything that this house contains of furniture, antiques, pictures, and bitter and sweet days, are all essence for her memories.

She refused anyone to participate with her in cooking, and bragged about what her hands would make. The days brought us closer until she willingly waived her responsibilities, and I began to do all the duties of the house and manage its affairs on my own, except for the cooking.

I began to feel more love and respect for her, but her condition while she was preparing food was difficult for me. She did not allow me to take this task from her... One day, she seemed tired, and her face was clearly weak, so I dared and said to her:

-        What do you think if you taste today a dish made by me?
She smiled, unconcerned with what I was saying, then I added:

-        Try me this time, if you don't like it, prevent me from entering the kitchen.
She looked at me with her usual look, and said:

-        Do you know how to cook despite your young age?
I replied with confusion and anguish:

-        Yes, Madame, life is a school that teaches us lessons of sweet and bitter.
I looked at her facial features, and saw that she was kind and affectionate... She nodded and then said:

-        Where is your family, my daughter?

Her question made me feel as if I was slaughtered from vein to vein, so I said:

-       O Madame, my story is a pain in my heart that hurts so much.

The old woman said kindly:

-       As long as you are fine, do not be sad, but where are your family? Where are your family?

I replied:

-       I am alone in this country, with no help or support.

She said:

-       How did you get to this country?

I squatted down on the floor, as if I had found the sanctuary that would allow me to express my great sorrow, and I said to her:

Do you have a desire to listen?

She replied spontaneously:

-       We have all the time.

Before I begin to describe my tragedy, she turned to me and said:

-       Talking without a cup of coffee has no taste.

I hurried to the kitchen to make a pot of coffee in which sincere feelings were deeply seething, and then went back. As soon as I was about to start telling my story, the door knocked... I looked at her, and she nodded to open it:

81

-       Perhaps he is Bilal and his family. He called and told me that he will come. To make sure of the guest. I asked, and he replied:

-       Open the door.

Before he could complete his sentence, I knew from the voice that he was her son, Mr. Bilal, who had brought me to this house a few days ago with his family.

The old woman was delighted and she spread her arms like a high flying bird, saying:

-       Bilal, my dear... Welcome my beloved.

He embraced her and kissed her hand, then said:

-       We came to visit you to check on you and on your condition.

She turned to me and replied:

-       As long as I'm with Elham, I'm fine.

She continued:

My daughter, please, prepare the table. Then she turned her eyes to her guests and added:

-       Today you will taste the food of Elham, who volunteered to prepare the dishes.

I left time and space for family conversations, which I had been missing for a long time, and went to prepare the table, but unusually, I was eavesdropping, and the memories came to my mind. I remembered my mother and our neighborhood, with its narrow alleys, and appeared to me our old house with my chalk drawings on the walls. I remembered the "gutter" from the roof of our house in the winter days when rain water flooded our streets, we run with the neighborhood kids, we play with devilish games and we drown in the mud, and our old neighbor comes out in a reprimanded anger, and we run like rabbits, afraid of his tyranny.

These memories opened the imagination to nostalgia for images that I missed.

However, the voice of "Hajji" cut off the brainstorming of past memories when it came to my ears saying:

-Where's the coffee, my daughter?

In a fleeting moment, I prepared a tray of coffee and presented it to the visitors, then I went back to the kitchen to arrange the food in the refrigerator. As soon as I finished my tasks, I went out to the balcony of nostalgia, as I called it, and my eyes fell on Adnan while he was holding my baby with his soft hand. My heart almost felt its beats and filled with joy. It is the first time I have seen him from such a close distance, as if he was in my arms. I began to watch him with longing and a broken heart until he disappeared from my sight, as if the moments around me were a wedding in progress. I was satisfied with these fleeting opportunities that my eyes glimpse at him from time to time to check on him. I closed the door of my cell and went back inside to complete the process of cleaning the house and drying the dishes, since the visitors had left silently, so I checked on her as she sat in her bed reading the Noble Qur'an, and returned to the watchtower, which became my only refuge. The night had brought down its dark veil, so I looked at the street, perhaps it would come to me in a dream, to color my eyes with the features of my innocent baby face.

"You will meet people make you fall in love since they deserve nothing but this." - Shams Tabrizi

---

I am safe and secure today, and these are my real feelings which I have due to a good woman who embraces in her heart this abundance of tenderness.

Gradually, I started to have a distance from fear and anxiety attacks. My only concern was to collect the amount that Adnan asked me to bring in order to get my son back from him. I counted the money I had collected and saved over the months of my service in Mrs. Hind's house, and it was a little over a hundred thousand. The hope to meet my child became within a short period, so I still have to strive to collect the rest of the ransom in order to enter with Adnan in a bargaining project through which I can obtain my child and my divorce papers, and return to my country with a broken heart. Happiness after suffering got closer, for I have a stable income and a safe place. What I feared most was to envy myself for this blessing, since deprivation triggers in us the blessing of contentment and ignites peace and faith in our depths. The world is treacherous, but the good woman, Bilal's mother, considered me as her daughter.

I spent my night steeped in a dream that I could not put on paper with my child, until the morning breathed life. While I was in the kitchen, as usual, making my morning coffee pot, she slowly came to me and asked:

- My daughter, I see sadness existing in your eyes, what is your story?

I carried the coffee tray and sat in front of her with my heavy tears, to tell her the story of my pain and deprivation of my baby, while she started to calm and sympathize me. Since she got much sensitive for this matter, her tears flowed warmly, and said:

- How's that? Where are the doors of justice and mercy that do not intercede for the case of a young girl who suffered much pain and humiliation?!

She took a deep breath and gently wiped the tears from my cheeks, then said:

- Where are your family?

I answered her:

- I know nothing about them since I came to this country, since I forcibly moved to an exile that I did not choose, and I suffered pains which I neither expect nor deserve... Madame, I am a woman who was condemned to persecution for a sin she did not commit.

She got angry and said:

- This prejudice is not accepted neither by God nor by humans!!

I wiped my tears again, and told her:

-     Do you believe me? I miss my family so much. I miss my younger brothers.

The pious woman stood from her chair and was silent for a few seconds, then said:

-     Look, Elham, your tragedy hurt me from the bottom of my heart, and I will try with all my power to help you until you meet your child and return to your family. Which type of man is your husband??

My story and my suffering were the only concern of "Hajji" throughout the day, so she seemed unusually upset, anxious, and careful about my feelings. When evening came, the kind woman warned me not to stay long in my watchtower, the secret of which became known after that meeting in which I told her all my tragedies, and then she entered her room. I went out to my balcony, watching the street, which was empty of people, and then I entered and lay my tired body on the bed. I thought with myself and wondered if I had the right to have more dreams, or should I be satisfied with what I accepted from my destiny, for fear that the days would turn against me again? It is enough for me to be close to my baby! I don't want more now! Then, I felt sleepy so I fell into a deep sleep.

As soon as Mr. Bilal arrived the next day, "Hajji" asked him to dictate a letter to her daughter, Rana, who was residing in the country. He complied with her wish, and she stated to him the following:

My dear daughter...

After longing and contentment, I ask you for a favor for the sake of a woman who deserves clemency. Kindly, collect information about the house of Mr. Ahmed and his wife Maryam in Jamous area in the suburb of Beirut, and God will reward you, then provide me with any information you obtain, as I am very interested in this matter. After that, she continued the rest of the letter asking about the conditions of the family and the children.

After concluding, "Hajji" instructed her son to send the letter to his sister, Rana. It was only a few weeks before she got a reply from her daughter. Bilal was reciting the content of the response to her ears, and every time he finished one section to start another, I was eager to hear something about my family, and before the last chapter, Rana wrote:

(As for the issue of Mr. Ahmed and his wife, he is fine with his children, but concerning his wife Maryam, may God have mercy on her, she passed away after a severe suffering of illness).

The end of the answer went drop like a bomb, and I could not utter a single letter, as words dried up in my throat, as if it was my destiny to receive calamities without distress, as my mother left without her farewell. She left this world after a painful struggle with illness. I suffered spiritually, especially after I knew that my father got married after her forty days of death and did not wait a year at least to pass, and that another woman entered our house, whom I do not know, for men are brought up on selfishness.

The atmosphere of the house was overshadowed by a compelling silence, since we were shocked, so that the religious "Hajji" was stunned by the speech, and I was robbed by sadness to the isolation. I have always wronged my poor mother...I thought she had gotten rid of me and doubted that she had forgotten me, while she was wrestling with death and concealing the truth of her affliction.

Oh my God, so many misfortunes! I did not commit a fault or a sin to fall into all these calamities, for worry, pain and homelessness all of these have become the pillars of my life. What is the fate of my brothers? What is their fate?? How will they be with their stepmother??

That night of mine was not even equal to the previous nights of torment and pain, to the extent that my child was absent from my memory. Rather, sadness carried me to my memories in our house as we gathered around the eating "Tablieh", lying on the ground like chicks surrounded around each other. Questions about the conditions of my brothers came to my mind after a strange woman entered their house, and I began to realize the meaning of the presence and the tyranny of a stepmother, who is, in the end, the ruthless aunt.

Silence dominated each of us, so the kind old woman remained silent and sadness revealed in her eyes with great pity about my situation, while my tongue stopped speaking... A few days passed, there were no conversations between us except what was easy, and one day I asked her:

- "Hajji", for God's sake, help me, since I feel my heart burning, and I am worried about the fate of my brothers.

She looked at me sympathetically, and said:

- What's on your mind, my daughter?

I'm thinking of sending a letter to my father.

She said:

- A good idea, we will wait for Bilal to visit us.

I replied:

- It is not necessary, I can read and write.

She was surprised, and signs of astonishment were evident on her features, then she said:

- Are you educated?

I said to her:

- Yes, I was in a public school and I studied up to the ninth grade before they married me.

The face of happiness and bliss was revealed, as if she had discovered something of great importance. She said:

-	Come on, write, my daughter, and be sure that your letter will be handed to your father. I will assign this responsibility to my daughter, Rana.

I left the remnants of past and pain, squeezed my memory, and began to write my words on paper, searching for expressive meanings that shall affect my father.

I wrote a letter in which there were many strong feelings, and pictures of my childhood and my heart-broke for the loss of my mother, may God have mercy on her, and not being by her side in her last days. I also told him inside the letter about my circumstances, the brutality of Adnan, and how he threw me in the streets in countries that do not resemble me, and about my deprivation of seeing my son. In the letter, I stressed how much I missed his embrace and the arms of my brothers, and I pointed in a polite manner, referring to the new wife, hoping that she would be a support and compassion for my brothers.

Then I folded the letter and handed it to Bilal's mother, hoping that she would send it to her daughter, Rana. Days passed while I was missing and waiting to see my baby from behind the window, or to receive a reply from my father, but nothing happened, and I began to lose hope. Sunday came, when the family of Mr. Bilal arrived to the grandmother's house and where there were circles of pandemonium; This tells the grandmother what happened to him, and that informs her of what his mother bought him, as for the girl Basma, she sits like a queen near her mother, for she knows how much everyone loves since she is the only girl in the family...After lunch, I noticed that Bilal had put something into the pocket of the old woman baggy robe. Before the visitors left the house, "Hajji" stopped Basma and allocated a sum of money for her, then distributed sweets and chocolate to the two young children boys. The house returned to its stillness, quiet and far from all this fuss and tumult. I proceeded to rearrange the place after the children left it in a complete mess. As soon as I had finished my work, and as I was about to enter my room, "Hajji" called me, saying:

-    Come, Elham... Don't escape, my daughter.

My heart shivered since her way this time was different from the previous ones, so I asked her:

-    What's wrong with you "Hajji"? Did I do something wrong?

She said:

-    No, my daughter, rejoice, you have received a letter from your father.

I felt as if my heart had jumped and my hands were shaking. I took the letter from her to read its content, so that I might catch a glimmer of hope, even if it was far from me. The message was full of emotions, as my father began to narrate in a semi-slang language what happened to my mother after my departure, and the pain she suffered as a result of the disease, especially after they completely had no news about me, and that she left satisfied with me while she was repeating my name only. He told me also that when they went to the house of Adnan's family to check on me, they found no trace of them. They immigrated to Australia. My family got lost in the world and I lost them, waiting for a lost hope, until the letter came from Rana, may God reward her with good.

My father had sent a closed letter with the message that I knew from its content that his new wife is a divorced woman who has no children, and she is taking care of my brothers by the best duty, and God is witnessing that, so there is no need to worry, rather he advised me to take care of "Hajji" Um Bilal, as if God had compensated me due to the loss of my mother.

His message was pure, sincere, through which I felt safe today. I read it several times in a row, and I looked at the kind old woman who was contemplating me with a satisfied smile, then I said:

-    Have you heard, my affectionate one? May God compensate us with good.

I hurried and opened the envelope, in which it was a sum of money worth a million liras. I was about literally floating on air of joy and happiness, then I said to "Hajji":

-       Look at the amount I have.

She said:

-       It became easy, it only got complicated in order to be solved! My daughter, the door of happiness at first seems to be difficult to enter, but later it becomes easier! Go in and sleep well.

Out of joy, I entered my room and forgot to ask "Hajji" if she wants something from me, but of course she excused me since I was wandering on another planet, rather I was flying in the sky with the angels due to my amazement.

As usual, I finished the house chores early and then went to my balcony watching the street and the passersby. "Hajji" came and asked me to change my clothes after she changed her clothes, then she asked me to hold her hand since she feels so tight that she is almost suffocating, and she wants to walk outside far from the walls of the house. I complied with her orders and we went out for a leisurely walk.

We bought some fruits from this shop, and from there pieces of cloth, then we went to the butcher at the end of the street since she wanted to buy some chicken and meat which Mr. Bilal usually bought. I later found out that she wanted me to go out of the house to entertain myself. After dinner, I sat alone in my room to read my father's answer for the tenth time, waiting to fell asleep.

The storm of change blew, and within a few months my lifestyle changed, so I began to go out to the market until I forgot that I work in this house, which I consider the most precious thing I have in the world.

"Everything in the world starts small and then becomes bigger, except bad things, they start big, and then get smaller with time"- Imam Ali bin Abi Talib, Peace be upon him

The months passed quickly, and I was always watching my child from my balcony without drawing Adnan's attention, but winter was about to leave, schools were closed, and tomorrow Rana and her family would be among us.

Time came for Um Bilal to wait her visitors from Lebanon and to welcome them with cheers and joy.

After the warm welcome and hug, Um Bilal said:

-       Thank God for your safety... Praise be to God.

She began kissing her daughter and her grandchildren, and she seemed like she had lost her mind due to her great happiness. Then, she turned to me and said:

-       Elham, this is Rana, my only daughter, notice her humanity, kindness, and attractiveness of her beauty.

I came closer to our visitor from Beirut in order to kiss her hand for her favor with me. She patted my shoulder and said:

-       Good people exist at all times and in all places, Elham… The first one you must thank is Um Bilal. Otherwise, they would not have known about your story in Beirut.

The chants of joy were indescribable and the conversations were very long between the kind "Hajji" and her daughter and grandchildren, so the demands increased, but I was happy for the reunion. I left them in the salon and went into the kitchen to prepare lunch, especially the plates that the soulful Um Bilal had taught me...

Rana had tasted my plates and whispered to her mother with a smile:

-      Your food is delicious, Mom!

The religious "Hajji" replied with a smile:

-      These plates are done by Elham, and I swear to God that I did nothing. Since she entered the house, she brought happiness and joy into my life. We hang out together, sometimes we play "Barjis", and sometimes we go to the market.

Rana was astonished by her mother's words, and said:

-      Why didn't you tell me all these things, Mom? You become close this much? Now my heart is at ease, and I am no longer afraid of loneliness for you. Are you thinking of coming back with me?

"Hajji" was silent for a while, thinking, and then answered:

-      Never, my daughter, here I have spent my youth since I married your father. I lived in this land for sixty years, and I will not leave the same except to be buried in my country.

Rana's eyes welled up with tears, and she answered:

-      No... No... "Hajji", long life, Inshallah.

In the evening, we all gathered around Um Bilal, who kept telling us stories and wisdom, until we felt sleepy and entered the rooms. That day I gave up my room for the children and preferred to sleep temporarily in the kitchen. Everyone went into their neat and tidy rooms after I had arranged their stuffs for them. Rana could not believe what she saw, so that the next day she whispered in "Hajji's" ear:

\-   I envy you, mom, for Elham, I wish I could steal her from you to support me in the affairs of my house.

A giggle heard by the sweet Um Bilal, and she said:

\-   No one will steal Elham from me until her situation is stabilized, her affairs are settled, and her mind calms down. She will not take a single step outside the threshold of this home until she gets her child back, after which she is free to make the decision that suits her.

The words of the affectionate old woman were a balm to my heart since she had felt the pain of my condition, and she cured my bleeding wound, then the talk was silent for a few moments until Rana said:

\-   Do not be afraid, Elham, for God is with the patient, and that the night must pass and the sun will rise, for every knot has its own solution.

I left them so that they would discuss in private family conversations, and returned to my solitude. I secluded myself like a lonely cat, reviewing its feelings, emotions and scattered thoughts. I started imagining the face of my child who was stolen from me and from which I am separated by some street steps. I stood up and stared at my balcony, which I had turned into a watchtower, hoping to see him with his father while he was outside, to beautify my eyes, which are deprived of him, with the shadows of his steps, as he walks with a gorgeous look, holding his father's hand.

Minutes passed while I was waiting in vain, until the street was empty of its passers-by, the cats came out looking for their livelihood, and I was impatient to wait more. Sleepiness overwhelmed me and I felt a strong urge to close my eyelids since I was exhausted and tired. My heavy steps drove me to bed, due to the many services and demands, for I work all day, dividing myself between the demands of "Hajji" and the desires of Rana and the children. I lay down my body which is burdened with aches on the bed, gave my mind a short break, then I fell into a deep sleep...

My night was different from the nights I had before. It was the night of rosy dreams, as if my heart beat, while I was in a deep sleep, like a violin whose strings were playing romantic melodies, after a quiet drowsiness that brought me a peace of mind. All I lacked was the face of my child and his innocent hands to wipe from my forehead the anguish of thirst and deprivation.

I wished that the night which passed would not be like the rest, and become just a memory. When dawn sent its golden lights to tickle my eyelids, I got up before everyone else had woken up, and went out to the balcony to get some fresh air.

While I was observing the beauty of the sunrise, I spotted Adnan at the beginning of the street, so I hurried and hid so that he wouldn't see me. He was going to work, and on his face the features of brutality and injustice, strutting like a peacock which fan out his feathers, as if he were a sultan of his "stature". He is devoid of mercy, free of humanity, greedy, drowned in his psychological complexes.

When I saw him approaching the building, my body shivered with revolt and hatred against a man without a conscience, unaware of the sin and fault committed by him, not feeling the suffering of a mother who was unjustly deprived of her child and forcibly displaced from her home, and not sensing the bitterness of a wife who sought with all honesty to preserve her home without pressures, forgetting her dreams, her age and even her being.I felt pain and nausea, for seeing him was like a knife stabbed in my flank. I entered my room, trembling, terrified like a sheep being led to slaughter, crying out in fear.I pressured myself and my nerves and collected the pieces of my soul. What is the fault of this family for making them endure my worries and tragedies?! The kindness, consent and embrace of the old woman is enough for me, for today she is the light in my life, the image of the mother I missed, and the refuge of safety!

The house breathed life and the faces began to appear one after the other, in turn, to go around the old woman and to gain the blessing and satisfaction from her kind face. Furthermore, my plenty tasks began, from preparing the tray of the coffee pot, making the beds and hanging the "pajamas," then meeting the non-stop and endless demands.

While I was busy performing the tasks, I felt something strange in the eyes of those present, especially Rana and "Hajji", as if they were preparing to launch an idea for a project. I divided my time between welcoming Bilal and his family, and Rana's children who went to the "shop" located at the end of the street...The first step was the family gathering around the breakfast table, which Rana helped me to prepare, and added a little of her taste to the style of the vegetable dish. "Hajji" who was sitting on the top of the table said:

- Listen to me children, today we decided to spend a long day on the riverside in the middle of nature, to reunite the family.

The children screamed so loudly so that the paintings hanged on the walls almost fell, and they entered their rooms crazy, collecting their toys and their needs, while Rana and I ran into the kitchen to prepare supplies of food and drink for the wilderness, in addition to choose comfortable clothes. Barely an hour had passed when it was all set up and everyone was ready to go out. Rana suggested that we take two cars for everyone's comfort, and she did what she suggested. While we were putting our needs and camping equipment in the two cars, the moments of memories popped into my mind, as if I went back ten years, to past days, particularly for the day off at the end of the week at the end of every month, when my father used to take us to Al Zahrani River in our dear South, taking what was delicious from food and drink, and how we used to go around my mother like chicks while she was preparing meat for barbecue. We were a kind family, just like "Hajji's" family, and it was filled with tenderness and love. On that day, I was eagerly waiting for the vacation and striving to complete my homework to have fun free and without restrictions. I later realized that my mother's initiative for my marriage to Adnan was not a bargain, but rather resulted from her fear for me, and all she wanted was to be assured of my future.

We went on and the road was rugged, crooked, with many bends and bumps, and at every turn I grabbed the kerchief of "Hajji", who was looking at me harshly with a blame smile, as if she was admonishing me, saying:

- The girl who was raised in the village must not be afraid! Despite the long distance and the journey, we did not feel bored, especially when "Hajji" unleashed her melodious voice by singing Mawawil, Ataba and Mijana, which touched my feelings, so I controlled my tears for fear of being exposed.

How difficult it is to emigrate and be separated from the parents, and the hardest feeling is when a mother is absent! We arrived at the destination and had to stop the two cars a short distance away since the road became impassable.

We got off and walked like nomadic gypsies, each of us carrying what he could, while Rana was looking for a suitable yard to camp in, until she found the right place.

We sat on the ground and the grass was still wet, while the water murmured like music, as if we were listening to a symphony of classical music... What a wonderful place where nature falls asleep on views that are almost paintings that no painter can paint! Pandemonium, fun, screaming and demonization... The children were happy with their freedom, filling the air with their laughter and giggles and even screaming as if they were prisoners who had just breathed a breath of freedom. Each of us went to carry out his task.

103

Only "Hajji" lay on the ground and leaned her back, then started weaving stories of the past with her crochet hook, while I was busy collecting wood and dry sticks to light the fire and prepare the barbecue grill. The children gathered around me, and some of them volunteered to help me in order to kindle the fire, while the beautiful and charming Haifa was helping her mother in sticking the pieces of meat with the barbecue skewers.

After finishing the task of kindling the fire, I began to prepare all kinds of salads. The most wonderful thing about this task was the idea of washing vegetables in the river, with the cooperation of everyone, even Mr. Bilal. We prepared a table full of spices and dishes that whetted the appetite of all to eat... "Hajji" turned to me with a cursory look and then nodded with her hand, so I came closer to her and listened while she whispered saying:

-       Elham, my daughter, there is nothing more delicious than a cup of coffee after lunch on the flame of this blazing coal.

Arabic coffee which is boiled on charcoal can boost the mood.

I patted her shoulder and winked that I understood her request. After lunch and the children had left to play, I brought her a tray of coffee as she had ordered, and poured her a large cup that brought up a smell of its fresh coffee. Rana was confused, and this was evident on her features, but she broke her confusion when she spoke to "Hajji", saying:

-        A beautiful trip, tenderhearted, and here is the family around you.

The old woman held back her tears and turned to her only daughter, saying:

-        My daughter, moments of happiness are very short, and for a long time happiness did not knock on my door. Coming with the kids this year brought me back to life. I felt that I was not interested in the day of departure after I made my eyes close to seeing you, and when God takes his deposit, I will close my eyes satisfied with you.

Rana bends down and kisses her pure hand, then raises her eyes while tears on her cheeks, so "Hajji" wiped her tears gently and said:

-        Don't cry, dear, this is the reality of life. Each of us has a time to go to a better place, so don't be late to come next time.

Rana tried to interrupt her, saying:

-        Mom…

"Hajji" prevented her from speaking with her fingertips, while saying:

-        My daughter, today you are a mother and you can understand the feelings of motherhood.

She hugs her tightly, and I feel an urge desire to hug my child. The mother, no matter how tender she is, she always has a hope to give more.

Before the night and the darkness fell on the place, we picked up our stuff to go back home. The way back was quiet and silent, especially since some of the children fell asleep, while others were still deepening in the ecstasy of this long day.It was an exhausting day for everyone, as we raced to bed, and we all fell into a deep sleep. The summer vacation is over and it is time for the children to enter school, so the travel bags have been prepared again. The holiday passed in the blink of an eye; farewell is very hard for Um Bilal, and it is more difficult to say farewell to the one we love. So, she controlled herself and seemed strong and solid, while Rana was busy packing the return bags, and silence dominated the place since they were sad. The arrival of Bilal changed the atmosphere while he was transporting bags and luggage by himself to his car, so the "Hajji's" eyes looked full of pain.

Rana and the children left, while the house embraced the memory of their laughter and frivolity, and drowned into a painful silence. Even talking between us abandoned the place, and "Hajji" returned to the nostalgia of her hook and crochet to kill the feelings of loss and separation, however, I returned to clean, wipe and wash as if what happened yesterday was a dream.

The routine dominated each one of us, and I returned to wait my son on my balcony as usual, perhaps he would pass by stealthily in front of my eyes.

Two years passed in a jiffy while I was in "Hajji's" house. Kamal's features became like a fantasy running against the clock. Today, my son ends a new year, and his childhood dreams blossom on the beginning of his three years.

Today, he has become a young man who can distinguish between his original mother and his stepmother, for this day has become engraved in my being, and I will not let it pass by, I will celebrate his birthday for the first time as if he were in my arms.

Yes, I'll make for him a party, prepare a candy cake and buy him a gift. Today, I can financially celebrate his birthday. It is the first time that I own a house and money that enables me to celebrate his birthday, since my previous circumstances in Hind's house would not have allowed me to celebrate with my beloved child. Today, I will bring him back by my feelings, my heartbreak and my pain, to put a kiss on his forehead, and say to him:

-       Happy birthday, my love... My life.

Despite suffering deprivation, I placed hope on a thin thread of faith, and relied on God to bring him back to my heart.I was working in the service of "Hajji" with all my heart and waiting for the moments to peek at my child who lives near my place of residence, and see him grow from a child into a young man.Every time I saw him from afar with his stepmother, my heart almost jumped out of my chest and excited to embrace him. He's a little man, and now he is carrying his schoolbag on his back and jogging the street on his first day of school. When I saw him, I lost control of my temper and ran to "Hajji" for giving me permission to leave. She seemed to understand what I meant, so she accepted. I went out into the street and followed him like a thief, watching his walk, his steps, his looks. The school is not far from home, and now it is open for the first day of the school year. He was not like the rest of the children of his age, crying and catching their parents, but he seemed confident of himself, understanding the place he was visiting for the first time. I was so close to him that my hands were about to touch his hair, and my arms could embrace him.

I hid behind a tall tree trunk for fear that his stepmother would see me, and I stared at my little sweet baby. He looked handsome and charming, with wide eyes and a thin body, with two dimples on his cheeks. I was noticing the maturation that occurred from day to day...They entered the school where the Head of the Nursery Department, apparently, greeted them, and the wife stood and spoke to her, then bent down and dropped a kiss on his cheek and walked away, so he waved at her with his innocent little hand saying goodbye. I waited behind the tree and the sun was covering me in its high heat, forgetting my job, the time and the place until after noon, when the parents returned to gather around the school fence, waiting for their children to come out. I took a step hoping that I could hug him, but I took two steps back since Adnan came up and stood in front of him, and the responsible handed him the hand of my child so that they could come home together. The schedule was that Rose shall take the child to school in the morning, and Adnan shall bring him home in the afternoon.

I went back and told "Hajji" what had happened to me, and she was shocked and seemed sad for what I was going through. She thought of me badly for being late, thinking that I would never come back again.

I gave her a blaming look, and said:

-       Never, Mom. I will not leave you no matter what happens, you are the safety that surrounds me and I live thereby.

The word unintentionally preceded me, so she embraced me, tightened me to her heart and gave me a satisfactory kiss on my forehead. The kind old woman returned to the subject, and asked me:

-       Tell me, my daughter, what happened to you in detail.

I told her how I felt when I saw him on a very short distance from me, and how his stepmother had thrown a kiss on his forehead. She interrupted me a little and then said:

-       Look Elham, perhaps this is a good beginning for you, so don't pre-empt things, for Kamal is in his third year and should be at school, then you must not be sad. Apparently, this woman treats him well. This angel shall not be blamed for what his father did. Let time prepare the events, and let your faith be strong in the Lord of the Worlds, for Allah gives respite, but never neglects.

111

Actually, what she said was true, and this is a perfect opportunity from which I can benefit in my favor, so that it shall help me see and check on my child on a daily basis. Instead of using the balcony as a watchtower, I could now turn the trunk of that tall tree into a haven to watch him closely.

Oh my angel! What a cool kid when you go to school! I am dying to embrace you, to hold you in my arms, and to open my heart and imprison you therein. Today I am related to you, and I am reassured about your condition since your stepmother treats you with kindness and tenderness, as if she is maintaining the trust so that I can recover it.I became persistent to hide in my haven every day, indifferent to the sun or storms, resisting the revolution of nature in all its vicissitudes. My only concern was to check on my little angel every day, and if one day I was too busy to go, "Hajji" would call and order me to go see him.

The school year passed quickly, and the school was about to close after nine months, where I did not stop for a moment when I could see him. I watched him daily either from my balcony, or hidden behind a tree, waiting to see him from afar.

I entered the fourth year of "Hajji's" service, where weeks and months of deprivation and separation passed with torment and pain, and where the sum of five million became ready. At the end of each month, when I received my salary from "Hajji", I sat on my bed and count my money as I count the days that separated me from my sweet little baby. Now, the meeting day has become very close and so the relief. Happiness looked like a horseman appearing after a long wait and patience.

The decisive fateful day came, when Mr. Bilal went to the school administration of Kamal, and asked them to allow me for seeing him, provided that Adnan must not know. I strengthened my determination, accompanied by "Hajji" Um Bilal, and we headed to school.My body was trembling like a bird afraid of flying, my steps were very heavy, and my thoughts and obsessions ran through my head, and I almost felt faint, however, the encouragement and insistence of "Hajji" on this meeting, which I considered the confrontation of fate, helped me to withstand and recover my strength.

The general director of the school was a man of integrity, his heart softened for me when Mr. Bilal informed him of my tragedy, and the presence of "Hajji" in this situation warmed his heart, so he brought the angel. He was a young, elegant, handsome young man. My heart started dancing with joy when I embraced him in my arms, with flesh and soul, and I began to feel my pain from his innocent breath and dropped my warm kisses on his forehead and on his two little palms.

I put him on my lap, while he was surprised, and whispered:

-        I'm your mother, Kamal!

The words vanished in my throat and the tears poured out, and I almost couldn't control this shiver that I felt, so the director took the child out of my arms, while "Hajji" started to caress his hair with the palm of her hand. I became detached from my reality and lost consciousness, but the principal insisted on returning him to class before the bell rang.

I followed him while he was at the door and told him:

- Kamal, my love, don't tell your father about our meeting, for I will come again to see you, my life, and then I kissed his forehead with a warm farewell kiss.

The director was shocked by the reunion, so he promised me to see him again, while my little angel was surprised by what was happening to him, and his little mind could not comprehend the truth and understand the injustice and cruelty of his father.

The real suffering is to control the feelings, since any reckless step could deprive me of seeing the child forever.

When I came home, I was another woman who came back to life, and my heart was beating fast. Without any thought, I found myself crawling on my knees to kiss the feet of "Hajji", which pulled me out so fast, saying:

- I seek refuge in God, Elham, what are you doing, my daughter? I didn't do any favors for you, I feel how you feel.

I hugged her tightly and said while crying:

\-   I saw him, Mom! I touched him and felt his breath, isn't he handsome? "Hajji" patted my shoulder and said:

\-   He looks a lot like you, as if I see you as a child in his age.

I came again this time to watch him from afar, perhaps something had happened, or perhaps the child had broken his promise and informed his father. Every time he entered the school gate, after his stepmother had left, he turns left and right while holding his teacher's hand. The situation remained calm and quiet for three weeks, until "Hajji" and I decided to visit him again, and my child was a solid man who kept his promise. When we entered the room of the director, who welcomed us warmly, "Hajji" asked him:

\-   How did it go, professor?

He replied with a smile:

\-   Praise be to God the boy kept his promise and did not tell his father, and things seem to be moving towards reconciliation.

"Hajji" thanked God and the director who ordered someone to bring the child.

In a few seconds, Kamal was on my lap, while I started kissing him and playing with him, then I asked:

\-   Tell me, my life, did you inform anyone about the meeting?

He replied:

-       No, I didn't tell anyone!

Well, my little boy, you are a good man, tell me, do you need something that you would like me to bring to you?

He hugged me tightly and said:

-       Yes... I want you to take me with you.

I lost control of myself again and my tears fell profusely, but I was afraid for him, so I controlled my temper and answered him:

-       Don't worry, my angel, we'll get back together and you'll come to live in my house, and we'll complete our life together... OK?

He smiled innocently, as sweet-smelling balm, and he said:

-       Yes... I agree, don't be late, Mom... I'll miss you.

I hugged him tightly and replied:

-       Make sure you keep the secret, and don't tell anyone about our meetings, and I promise you that I will arrange things and we will be together.

The time for the visit was over and the director came to take him to his class, but Kamal turned back and ran towards me to put a kiss on my cheek and to wipe my tears with the palm of his hand.

"If I had had the power to prevent my own birth, I should certainly never have consented to accept existence under such ridiculous conditions."-Dostoyevsky

---

I began to recover my entity as a woman, after passing a long period fraught with difficulties and obstacles. Four years after my immigration to the African continent, I became more capable of everything than before, and the female within me is now able to withstand, take revenge and destroy any obstacle she encounters. Today, I have become a mature mom and a conscious woman, and between the two, a woman who is revolting against circumstances, place and time, dwelling in me. I was spending the time to plan for a safe future path with my child, away from Adnan's selfishness, brutality, and tyranny. He is no longer present in my memory, as the days I lived with him have been erased from my memory and I consider that he has become among the dead who were burned by the fire of their grudges.

Today, I live on the hope of meeting my child, my angel, my guardian and my future man. All that matters to me is to secure him a happy life and an unlimited kindness. I now have enough money to negotiate with a greed and spiteful husband. The sum of the money I saved now exceeds five million, which Um Bilal often supported me with. She always gave me tips, with or without a reason, adding them to my salary.She was giving me what she had saved from her son Bilal so that I could resist and have my baby. She was a real mother to me, she took care of me with all the tenderness and affection until I couldn't leave her for a second, and if I could make her a favor, I would give her my eyes and scarify my soul. I thank you, God, for you have been generous with me, you have freed me from the clutches of loss and the lust of human wolves, and turned my pain into a way out for a better life. I was happy until things began to change. An urgent problem appeared when "Hajji" began to feel unwell from time to time, and the treating doctors were ordering her to enter to the hospital and to perform some necessary medical analyses for her. At that time, the problem began to get more complicated, especially when she was suffering from a shortness of breath, so she seemed like a slaughtered bird fluttering in the bed, while I was unable to treat her. She can no longer dispense with nebulizers since her condition is getting worse, and her asthma is rapidly deteriorating.

Her health began to collapse and her condition worsened, until her physician ordered her transfer to the hospital, so she accepted. Mr. Bilal asked to secure a bed for me next to hers after her health deteriorated daily, which led the doctor finally to put an artificial respirator for her. In a short period, signs of thinness on her body began to reveal, and she became tired and her strength betrayed her, so she could no longer eat her meals, and she started sleeping more than usual. My heart was pounding and my mental health was destroyed, due to the continuous deterioration of "Hajji's" health day after day.

Today I woke up to an unusual movement. "Hajji" is in a complete coma, and the doctor asked Mr. Bilal to come early, and the nurses are working like bees, where every minute one of them enters to hand over the tasks to another. I approached her bed and wiped her forehead with a tissue, but she was asleep and had no contact with the outside world. I came closer to her and whispered in a low voice:

- "Hajji", can you hear me? If you can hear me, squeeze my hand.

She extended her hand heavily, and tightened my hand through her fingertips.

Tears preceded me and I was afraid to believe my thoughts, but the coming of Mr. Bilal brought me back to my consciousness. As soon as the physician entered the room, he ordered me to leave, and he remained with Mr. Bilal. It was only a few seconds until I noticed a rush of nurses and many medical devices being entered into the room, as if the large hospital had become inside this narrow room. At the end of the corridor, I caught sight of Mr. Bilal's wife, who was approaching in panic, as if what was happening predicted bad news.

Everyone is nervous, the door is closed and no creature is allowed to enter the room, and Mr. Bilal's wife began to read the Qur'an, while I was standing in the midst of this commotion confused, wrestling with suspicions, refusing for the matter to happen. Minutes passed, until the storm calm down. The nurses came out gloomy and sad, and I saw the staff returning their artificial respirators equipment downstairs. Mr. Bilal stepped out with tears on his cheeks, while the doctor remained in the room with the Head of the Nursing Department. The statement ended... Yes, the statement ended, and for a moment I did not comprehend the truth of what happened, and before he uttered his usual phrase:

- It's over, "Hajji" passed away!

I screamed a voice that almost penetrated space, as if this voice insisted on accompanying her pure soul, then I fell unconscious, so the nurses rushed to my rescue. When I regained consciousness, I asked the doctor, with a special request, to enter her room alone. After a bitter insistence, he allowed me to do so. I entered the room while she was lying on the bed, and her face was covered with her white veil; I lifted it up and stared at the features of this pure face...She was asleep like an angel, and her usual smile was hidden behind a skin as fresh as a baby's one, while her hands were open. I knelt and kissed her feet, afraid that my tears would fall on the corpse, then whispered while I was crying in a broken heart:

120

-        Why did you leave so early, Mom?... Why, my God?
Good people leave secretly, take our pains and pass away. There is no might nor power except with Allah. No objection to his will!

Unexpectedly, a nurse's hand extended to my shoulder, pulled me out of the void that had resided inside me to wake me up from my coma and to order me to go out, since they would prepare the corpse according to the Shari ceremonies, so that she will be washed and shrouded.

"Hajji", who opened the door of safety to me has gone away...She left to the world of eternity before I took my child back, and before I gave her part of her favor, so I returned to hell again. I lost my mind and started slapping my face like a madwoman, talking to myself, calling her so that she might answer the call. The pure-hearted woman who compensated my deprivation has disappeared, and complaining to someone except God has become humiliating, for I breathed the breezes of hope from her satisfaction and embrace. I lived the faith within the purity of her white veil and the rhythm of her crochet hook. She was my home, my sanctuary, and my pain balm. I lived with her for four years while I was secured and happy.

The corridor began to buzz with the expats from the Lebanese, and Mr. Bilal seemed very sad for a heart that was eager to provide him with happiness. Each of them was devoted to his duties, and how to transport the corpse to Beirut, and to prepare for the funeral and burial ceremonies. Tomorrow was fixed as a travel date, since in order to honor the dead, you must bury him. It was hard for me to comprehend her passing.

Without a purpose, I found myself wandering the streets with tears rolling down my cheeks, searching for her among people's faces, for her pure face that was my support in my loneliness, my crisis and my pain, this face that lit a candle in my darkness and sent a light to my salvation. I was distracted, so I laid my head on an old wooden chair on the sidewalk facing Hajji's house. I was tired and sleepy. I imagined myself inside the house in the dark, but I was afraid to turn on the light so that I could lose her shadow. I imagined her sitting on the same chair weaving her crochet, or on the balcony watering the planting basins. I saw myself entering her room and the bed was empty. For the first time, I couldn't find her sitting there reading the Noble Qur'an. A terrible feeling when we lose who we loved, so that death will be treacherous and compelling, especially when all things stay as they are, even her glasses on the table, her rosary and her prayer rug.

This is the tragedy, and this is the life that has become the shroud that Adnan gave me. Honestly, I spent a very difficult night with Um Bilal, for I feel that her spirit is with me. I hear her, I touch her, and I am afraid that she will leave me. I was afraid to wake up from that dream to return to the agony of the fact of her departure.

I woke up from my delusion and realized that I was imagining things, and that the brunt of the catastrophe and its horror affected my psyche, as I could not enter the house since the key was with "Hajji", may God have mercy on her, so I spent the night on the sidewalk facing the building. I came to the house again, but the door was locked, so I lay down on the threshold in front of it. However, I felt her presence inside, as if her soul was surrounding me with safety. At noon, I lost my patience and went to the tree trunk in front of the school, perhaps I could see my child while he was leaving, but in vain. I had a deep sense urging me to go home again, since I haven't showered for two days and I felt disgusted with myself. I was afraid of being stranded again in the streets, and of losing the hope of getting my child back. I returned like a homeless cat, and sat in front of the door, waiting for her to open and to give me a hug.

I hated self-pity and no longer believed in fate, for whenever safety and happiness knocks my door, it shocks me again with obstacles, calamities, and horrors that no soul can bear.

While I was communing with God, to solve my problem, I felt a strange hand patting my shoulder, so I got up in a panic, seeking refuge with God, whereas Mr. Bilal was standing in front of me and wondering my presence in front of the door, so he questioned:

- Elham, where have you been? How did you disappear from us? "Walaw"?

I lost words and excuses. Only my tears were the sure answer, so he completed his questioning:

- We searched for you for so long, why did you leave the hospital in a hurry? The words got stuck in my throat, and I answered him in a quivering, intermittent voice:

- The one who was kind to me and who embraced me passed away, and I am a helpless woman who has no power. The departure of "Hajji" weakened me... Shocked me... Look Mr. Bilal, I have been away from my country and my family, and I have endured the agony of my mother's separation, my suffering, my wounds, and the deprivation of my child, only since "Hajji" gave me strength and patience.

He opened the door, then looked at me and said:

- Do not despair, Elham, for "Hajji" has left the body, but it is always with us. Whoever she loved and honored in her life, we will love and honor him. You have become part of the family. I have my sister, Rana, and now I have a second sister, who is similar to her. "Hajji" has recommended to take care of you, and we are faithful to her will. Come to my house, the family is waiting for you.

I tried to control myself and to stifle the cry inside me, but I couldn't, and I started crying like a little child, while Mr. Bilal said to me:

-       Cry as much as you want, Elham, for crying is the best cure for the soul, as it purifies it from torments.

How difficult is parting and how harm is the injustice of life! You see how it mess with us when we become adults, while we used to mess with it when we were young. The real expectation in people's hearts varies from one person to another, since I experienced and discovered in the heart of Mrs. Hind and her husband an absolute dehumanization, and a selfishness that cannot be described in words, whereas I touched a flood of humanity, favor, kindness and emotions in the heart of "Hajji" and her family, and I saw the life in eyes of the pious. Shiny social appearances, covered with hypocrisy and deception, will no longer be able today to deceive me, and I become a predatory woman in order to continue my struggle, especially after the departure of "Hajji" that broke my heart and allowed the fear to encroach my being.

I regained the hope that I had lost when I parted from "Hajji", and the words of Mr. Bilal came like rain to refresh the soul and to control my heartbeat, for the storm could not destroy me, and what the devils have manipulated with me, I will defeat them by God's permission.

We entered the house, while the shadows of her soul inhabited it, as if she had not left. Everything was still the same. Her only pastime crochet, her glasses and her white veil. I picked the veil up and smelled jasmine, her favorite perfume. I imagined life crumbling like mirrors, and thoughts dying in fear of tomorrow. I yearned for that dreamy girl who used to draw her happiness on her school notebook, longing for the tenderness which was stole by time. I missed the sound of "Hajji" as it awakens peace in my soul and repels homelessness, for I am still searching for things that belong to me that I do not know and other things that I miss, and my only concern is my child and the moment of his return to my heart. While I was plunging in these emotions, the voice of Mr. Bilal brought me back from my wanderings when he asked me:

- What's wrong with you, Elham, don't you want to pack your stuff? Come on hurry up please!

I rushed to my room to pack my stuff, and I saw the door of the balcony overlooking the building in which Adnan lives, was open. I stood and looked away, hoping to glimpse my child for the last time before parting led me to another side of life. We walked together without words, not even whispers, while tears

126

were shedding on my cheeks like rain, and Mr. Bilal was walking with heavy steps as if he was tired and sad.

The family was together. As soon as we entered, Mrs. Suzanne was surprised by my presence, and she goggled her eyes and asked him:

- Where did you find her, Bilal?

He took a deep breath and replied:

- She was on the threshold of the house of "Hajji", may God have mercy on her.

She looked at me with a lot of bewilderment and blame, then said:

- What is your secret, Elham? Why didn't you come to us? We've been looking for you everywhere.

I replied:

- Forgive me, Mrs. Suzanne, my mom's passing for the second time touched me and broke my heart.

She hugged me gently and said:

- May God forgive you for this act, for everyone considers you a member of the family. The religious old woman, may God have mercy on her, recommended to take care of you.

We walked together to the sitting-room, while Mrs. Suzanne had entered the kitchen for a few seconds and then came back with a cold glass of juice, then said:

\-   Drink this glass of juice and rest, you look tired.

I asked them:

\-   Has the corpse of the good-deed woman arrived to Beirut?

Mr. Bilal held his feelings and replied:

\-   Yes, my brother did the funeral...I was told that a big funeral was made for her.

I burst into tears, whereas Mrs. Suzanne calmed me down, and then said:

\-   May God have mercy on her, she loved you like her daughter Rana.

I wiped my tears with my sleeves, and said:

\-   God is witness to my love for her. She was my mom, my friend, and the affectionate cuddle to me in exile.

Mrs. Suzanne hugged me again, and said:

\-   We are also your family and your people. We will fight with you to get your only child back and to secure a better life for you both. Do not be afraid.

Mr. Bilal emptied his pocket and said:

\-   Elham, you have with me a trust that was recommended by "Hajji".

He put a closed envelope, and continued, saying:

- This is an amount of money that the religious old woman, may God have mercy on her, had saved for you, so do not open it now, you have plenty of time later.

Then he stood up and went to his room.

Mrs. Suzanne, with her great generosity, invited me to enter the kitchen and choose the lunch dish according to my taste. Then she came back and followed Mr. Bilal. She tried to make me feel safe and that I am truly part of the family. In the evening, silence prevailed throughout the house and everyone entered his room, but Mrs. Suzanne kept watching a dubbed TV series, so she called me and said:

- Why are you prisoning yourself in the kitchen? Come, for the sake of God, and follow the events of this series with me. She insisted a lot, so I brought her a cup of tea and sat in front of her. I stared at her features, and all what I have found was kindness and an intimacy spirit blowing from her.

The series ended, and she turned off the TV and directed me to the room she had allotted for me. I stretched out on the sofa and opened the envelope that Mr. Bilal had given me. I was astonished and amazed. It was an amount that is beyond need and imagination, worth two million and perhaps more.

The woman passed away highly concerned about me, leaving a large amount of money to help me get my child back and get rid of Adnan's tyranny.

Daydreams began to grow deep in my depths, and I felt a joy that my words could not describe, but I controlled myself since we were in a sad atmosphere. I stayed up all night praying for her pure soul and reading verses from the Noble Qur'an and Doaa (supplication) that shall warm her grave and shrouded her with contentment. The hours passed quickly, whereas dawn shone with golden rays, and life returned to the house. Mr. Bilal was the first to enter the living-room, and he found me sitting reading the Noble Qur'an. I saw a hard tear in his eyes, so he came to me and said:

-       May God reward you, my sister!

His words warmed my heart, and I felt the sincerity of his brotherhood, so I hastened to prepare a pot of coffee for him, while Mrs. Suzanne joined him after a few seconds. She glanced in a hurry, and he told her what he had just seen. She nodded her head that she had seen me, then she greeted me with a smile, and said:

-       Good morning! "Tell me Bilal", is there anything more beautiful than the family?! May God bless our family.

- He smiled and said: Ameen.

It was a decisive day, since Mr. Bilal was traveling to Beirut to stand with the family at the funeral. His wife and I cooperated in packing his suitcase, and escorted him to the door where the taxi was waiting for him, hoping that he would arrive safely, and Mrs. Suzanne insisted he calls her the moment he arrives at Beirut Airport to rest assured.

"Keep on asking, and you will receive what you asked for. Keep on seeking, and you will find. Keep on knocking, and the door will be opened to you" - Jesus, peace be upon him.

My first days were weary at Mrs. Suzanne's house, since I had not yet gotten used to the atmosphere, especially since the owner of the house threw the burden on me to discover things and their locations by myself. At noon, the children came back from school, had lunch, and then went back to do their homework. It was necessary to prepare the "hubble-bubble" since Mrs. Suzanne is fond of the "Ajami Narghile" and prefers it in moments of serenity. I also prepared a pot of coffee, and we sat in the living-room. The owner of the house noticed a perplexing issue in my eyes, so she asked me:

- Do you have anything you would like to disclose, Elham? As if she had read my thoughts, so I settled down in my seat and said:

- You know that "Hajji", may God have mercy on her, left me a sum of money to help me get my child back to my arms, and I am waiting for Mr. Bilal to return safely to guide me to the path of negotiation with my husband, since I feel unable to face him alone.

She took a sip of her coffee, and said:

-       Thank you for this coffee. Never worry, since the family lawyer will take care of this case, and there is no power in the world that can deprive a mother of her son.

My tongue stuttered and I was unable to thank her, so she took the initiative and said:

-       Do not be afraid. Tomorrow I'll call him and let him know your case.

Mrs. Suzanne went out to the outer garden of the house to inform Um Rabih, the driver's wife, that she wanted to talk to her husband as soon as he returned from the market. I was overwhelmed with feelings that words cannot describe, as if I were breaking all the chains that prisoned me in the dungeon of oppression and persecution, and I became like a bird that abandoned its cage after years of oppression, then spread its wings soaring in the space of freedom.

Your mercy, God! How great is your mercy! What comes after hardship is ease, and here I am on a date with fate to meet my child, to hug him again and to touch his skin, face, and hair. The driver, Abu Rabih, appeared before Mrs. Suzanne, where she requested him to go to the Office of the Lawyer Mr. Joseph Abdo, who is one of the eminent lawyers, and to inform him of the necessity of his coming.

Abu Rabih hurried to carry out the mission. In the meantime, I got to know the house corner by corner, and I began to identify the places of groceries and cleaning tools. The work for Mrs. Suzanne is not tiring and exhausting, but my feelings are always longing for "Hajji" that embraced me with the tenderness of a mother, and treated me with kindness and compassion. When I finished my tasks at home, my only entertainment was playing with the children: Karim, Raghad and Basma. The little girl Basma was really the smile of this house and its fragrant rose. She is very tender and compassionate, and she is capable of expressing her feelings despite her young age. She is witty and intelligent, behaving like mature adults. Mrs. Suzanne felt an indescribable serenity for her children, while they were happy and having fun as if she had never seen them in this condition before.

The noise subsided at the beginning of the night, and the children went to their beds after turning the lights off, whereas Mrs. Suzanne prepared her cup of coffee to watch her favorite dubbed TV series. I entered my room looking for glorious moments to fall asleep, but the task was very impossible since my dreams refused to leave, and these strong feelings in my heart refused to obey the orders of drowsiness, so I started to imagine the coming days as a white horse wandering in green and multicolor lawns, and bragging about the return of a lost son to his mother's arms.

My hands were clapping for joy without moving, and my body was dancing to the tune of a hope that was almost becoming real.

Kamal's picture used to come to me with every light shining towards me. I was breathing him with every single breath of mine. I see him coming to hear my complaint when my tired soul perishes to hold him in my heart, to break my tremendous sadness, to tear the sails of fear and to tell me about his childhood that lacks his mother's tenderness, that was my soul's thirst. Kamal, you are the one who owns the key to relief! You are the one I want to drink the cup of life with! O companion of the heart's claim, fate will not break me, No, I swear to God! I'll return myself back and disappoint my destiny!I will defend my continuity by steadfastness to finally bring you back to my heart! You are the scene of life, the winter of nostalgia, the call for the morning sunshine, and from your eyes I will create my new path!Your existence increased inside my heart, so that my soul leaves me daily due to yourseparation, and I die thousand times while you are still alive! I will cross the sea of sadness through the ship of hope and anchor in the port of the future, then I will leave behind me memories that do not resemble me, since I am tired of the falseness and pain of life. Your face will be the weapon of my next life! I will close the gate of sorrow, and fly with you to the future, opening the doors of optimism again! I will embroider you my next days! I will take you back and sue life, since I have endured death for you once, but I will not bear it twice.

At ten in the morning, I heard the ring of the doorbell, so I hurried to open it to see a handsome man in his fifties, who had a protruding mole on his cheek, with curly hair, and had some gray hair on his locks. He introduced himself to me as the Lawyer Mr. Joseph, and then entered the living- room. He seemed to me that he knew every corner of the house and that he feels more comfortable in the living-room than anywhere else. When I asked him of his favorite drink, until Mrs. Suzanne came, he smiled saying:

-        A cup of Turkish coffee.

Before I went to make coffee for him, he surprised me by asking:

-        Are you Elham?

I nodded Yes and continued toward the kitchen, while Mrs. Suzanne took advantage of these minutes and told him my story. I touched while giving him coffee glances full of enthusiasm and impulse, as if he had addressed me without uttering a word, so that these looks were considered to me as an understandable letter.

The owner of the house asked me to sit down and explain my problem in detail, so that Mr. Joseph would be fully aware of what I suffer from and familiar with the smallest details of the issue. I was narrating to him the facts; however, every time I went back to a memory, I felt a terrible suffocation, and my heart almost stopped beating. I was keen to tell in deep detail, until I thought for a moment that he was upset with my story. As for Mrs. Suzanne, she was listening and rubbing her hands as if she was suffering from a great obstacle. I got tired of difficult and devastating details which destroyed the dreams of a teenage girl who was drawing the horizon of her future with roses, and imagining the features of her lover as in stories and novels. I got tired of a time that restricted even laughter, displaced me on the roads and insulted me in the service of people, until I looked like a sheep strayed from her herd and lost in the forest of wolves, every wolf craving to devour a piece of my body. I saw tears in her eyes, as if she had plunged herself into the deep moments of my life, but her pride prevented these tears from falling, so Mrs. Suzanne seemed to me a symbol of humanity and its essence.

Mr. Joseph lit his cigarette, had a sip from his coffee, and asked me:

- Elham, in the midst of this tragic story, where was your family? Why did you not contact them??

I replied:

-        He prevented me from leaving the house totally. He exercised his dictatorship over a weak, young soul. He was a monster in the shape of a human.

Mr. Joseph went on and asked me:

-        We are in a country that respects the law, and rejects the law of the jungle. Why didn't you lodge a case against him in the courts?

I smiled while reprimanding life, and said:

-        How could I file a lawsuit when I came out of his house expelled without shelter or food, and homeless on the roads! Without the grace of "Hajji", may God have mercy on her, and her embrace of me, I didn't know where to go.

I could not hold back the tears that shed profusely. When I regained my breath, while he was staring at me, I continued, and said to him:

-        Mrs. Rana, may God protect her, reunited me with the family.

He took again a sip of coffee, continuing his questioning, then he said:

-        Do you want to get your child back today?

I contemplated the past and the present in the blink of an eye, and said to him:

-        I buried myself, I even forgot my birth date, and I only care about Kamal who I shall embrace and who shall live in my arms, in order to cure my eyes while seeing him growing up little by little.

He replied:

-        What are his conditions to release your child?

I told him:

-        He obliged me to pay five million pounds.

The Lawyer stood up, as if a genie had dressed him, and said:

-        He asked you for a ransom?

I told him in a stifled voice:

-        Right!

He sat down in a different mood, and confusion was evident on his features, so he rubbed his forehead with the tips of his finger, then sighed and said:

-        Well, don't worry, the law is on your side. The first step we will take is the Court to file an urgent case for child custody. Therefore, we will provide you with an adequate housing to legally support the case and to lawfully confirm your work in this house, in order to prove before the Court that you have an income that allows you to support your child.

Something prompted me to ask him spontaneously:

-        In case of refusal to give up the child?

He smiled as if he had mocked my question and replied:

-        Then, we will see what to do. The important thing is, do you have a birth certificate for the child?

I told him:

-        Of course not.

He said:

-        It is not a problem! I can get it from the hospital administration... What I request from you is to rest and be fully prepared tomorrow at seven in the morning.

I asked with confusion:

-        Is there a please, Mr.?

 He smiled back and said:

-        Inshallah, tomorrow you will accompany me to obtain a birth certificate from the hospital to prove parentage, and then we will draw a plan for any step we take. Tomorrow I will be at seven o'clock at the entrance of the building waiting for you. Do not forget to bring your identification documents, such as your passport or your identity card.

Here is the big catastrophe! In the blink of an eye, life became dark since my unjust husband had stripped me of everything. The Lawyer noticed my confusion and immediately understood that I did not have identification papers, so he turned his lower lip in regret, and knocked a little, then said:

-       No worries, we will communicate with your family in Lebanon to provide the necessary papers.

Mrs. Suzanne implicated herself in the conversation, and said:

-       There is nothing wrong! The issue is resolved! My husband is in Beirut, I will inform him of the matter to visit her family, to reassure them of her health and to bring all the necessary papers for her case.

Then Mr. Joseph left, and I entered the kitchen in a state of panic and great anxiety, fearing that my case would be hindered after this struggle. I lost in a deep abyss of black thoughts, and the worries came up to my memory until I fell asleep, so I lay down on the ground as a lifeless body. I didn't feel my presence until the morning when the children were getting ready to go to school. I woke up unusually, energetic and full of vitality.

Mrs. Suzanne surprised me to prepare myself to accompany her to the house of the late Um Bilal to make some arrangements thereto. My heart danced with joy since I would pass by the apartment where my child lived. Indeed, the road seemed short despite the long distance. I received orders from Mrs. Suzanne with a great happiness. I first started cleaning the house, washing the "blankets" and emptying the refrigerator. I was happy despite the many tasks. At noon, I took the opportunity to rest, so I entered my room and went out to the usual balcony, the gazebo, and I sat anxiously watching the street very carefully, hoping that Kamal would pass for a moment before my eyes.

I was tired of waiting, my eyes tired of observing faces, and I almost forgot the rest of the tasks to be done before it got dark, so I hurried inside and left my heart on the gazebo.

Sometimes our sincere feelings drive us to oases of hope surrounded by a high wall of anguish and longing, which inflames our emotions. Mrs. Suzanne came at sunset to take me back to her house, and I had an idea that I encouraged myself to say at the right moment. I was in a bitter struggle within me, as if I was drowning in the middle of the sea, struggling with death in search of his salvation. The idea imprisoned me in stormy emotions from which there was no way to escape. The storm subsided in the house, and the children finished eating their dinner, so they quickly changed their school uniforms and put on their pajamas, and each of them went to his room. I hurried to the kitchen, made a cup of coffee, and went back to the living-room, where Mrs. Suzanne was sitting, watching her favorite program. She caught my eye in great bewilderment, so she waited until the end of the program.

She turned off the TV and quietly turned towards me and stared at me for a long time, then said:

\-   Tell me what you have, Elham, I glimpsed a confused question in your eyes.

I was a little confused, and then I told her:

\-   An idea came to my mind, Mrs., during my meeting with the Lawyer Mr. Joseph.

She was amazed and said:

\-   An idea... What is it?

 I answered:

\-   What do you think if Mr. Joseph would exchange Adnan for the money he asked me instead of waiting for legal transactions in Lebanon?

She thought a little, then said:

\-   But it's very dangerous.

I replied:

\-   Never, Mrs.! I know Adnan very well. He is greedy and weak towards money.

She sighed and said:

\-   I know how sad your heart is for your child.

Before responding to her, my tears preceded me, so I said:

\-   You are right, I am very eager to get my child back and to embrace him, for being away from him breaks my heart.

She put her cup of coffee on the tray, and said:

\- Well, tomorrow morning, we'll call the Lawyer and consult him. Now go to sleep, for tomorrow is near.

Mrs. Suzanne entered her bedroom, while I remained on the sofa in the living-room. My eyes fell behind the window crystal, where silence dominated the place, as if the universe was mute. It is the night in which I kept my secrets and my sufferings, to which I entrusted my pains and hid my tears. I went back to my forgotten teenage years in that modest neighborhood in which I grew up, the day I went to my school carrying in my books pictures of my dream knight who came from the mist of the unknown, where the strings of memories started to play the sweetest feelings, so I imagined my mother when she was waiting for me on the balcony, like a sewing shuttle back and forth. If I was a little late, she would be crazy and unleash her tongue in reprimand and shriek. At that time, I used to hide my childhood secrets in my room, so I would rush thereto and shut the door on myself and dream…

I watched the moon as it disappeared little by little in space, as if it were taking my heart through this journey. The image of my only child was engraved in my memory and attached to the single moments of my life. A terrible feeling when we live our memories with pain, and a destructive feeling when life becomes hard on us, since injustice is one of the worst feelings that a person suffers.

144

I felt sleepy, so I leaned my head on the sofa, waiting for the moon to wake me up from my deep sleep, but it drifted away. The sun tickled my eyelids and I was exhausted from sleep, twisted on myself. I shook off the monotony of the dream and went to the kitchen to prepare breakfast for the family.

My day started at seven in the morning and didn't end until the end of the night. There was no time for my dreams, for I was a woman crowned with grief, and depriving me of my child increased my belief that escaping from the burden of pain strengthens and supports the strength of resistance in us.

I began to think of a plan by which I could persuade the Lawyer to reach a barter deal with Adnan, since I am now in a fierce battle to get my child back. All circumstances and conditions are intertwined, and it is very difficult to penetrate them, since the power is in the hands of Adnan, who is the definitive ruler in my suffering, and the decision to release my son must be pronounced by him alone.

My waiting time to meet the Lawyer again was long. It seemed like days, but the house tasks assigned to me by Mrs. Suzanne filled my time. At noon, the house bell rang, and I immediately knew that Mr. Joseph was the one at the door. I rushed and opened the door, however, he was surprised by Mrs. Suzanne's unexpected call, so he asked me:

- What's wrong, Elham, and why does Mrs. Suzanne call me to come in a hurry? I answered:

- You're welcome, Mr. She is waiting for you.

I made him coffee, and sat next to Mrs. Suzanne, who took the initiative to say:

- Mr. Joseph, you know how anxious Elham is to get her child back, and in order to achieve this in a short time, what do you think of her suggestion?

He turned to me and said:

- What is your suggestion?

I told him:

- Mr. Joseph…, my "honorable" husband wants money to give up custody of the child and my supporting papers, so I thought if you would enter into a barter with him in order to shorten the time.

He replied in a serious voice:

- What if he refuses to barter?

I gave him a sad smile, and said:

- I'm sure he'll agree, since he's not a straight man.

He took a quick sip from his cup of coffee, then said:

- To this extent he loves money?

I replied:

- Listen Mr., the only concern of "Adnan" is to abstain from his responsibilities and commitments as a husband. This man is the opposite of what he reveals to people, he is a wolf in the clothes of human.

The professor turned to the lady of the house and said:

- If the issue is a matter of money, then it is easy, but we have to wait to find a way to talk to him.

I said:

- What do you think if I accompany you to his house and propose to him the deal that he always wished? I only want my son and I have no intention of taking revenge on him, for I delegated my case to God and He is the one who can take my right.

The lawyer was surprised by my words, and replied:

- What do you think, Mrs. Suzanne, about what Elham proposes?

She replied with great enthusiasm:

- If the issue of barter is legal, then why not proceed with it?

He said directing his talk to me:

- Do you have the money, Elham, to complete this barter?

I told him:

\-   Don't be afraid of the financial issue, for I spent several years working in the houses to provide him with the required amount to get my son back.

He answered me:

\-   Do you know Adnan's times?

I answered him very firmly:

\-   Yes, I have always followed the timings of his leaving in the morning and his return in the evening from the balcony in the house of "Hajji" Um Bilal, may God have mercy on her, for he comes back between five and six in the evening.

Mrs. Suzanne said:

\-   In my opinion, it is not difficult.

He replied:

\-   Of course not…

He went on, saying:

\-   Prepare yourself at quarter to six, and be ready to accompany me to his house...

I felt as if I had entered heaven, not caring about what awaits me or how Adnan would receive me and Mr. Joseph. All what I was thinking about then was completing this fateful deal in my life. Finally, I would be free and I would take back my being and my freedom from the hands of a ruthless oppressor.

Mr. Joseph was punctual, and at six we went to Adnan's house. My steps were fast, racing the wind, and as soon as I knocked on the door, Adnan opened it, surprised and confused, then said:

-        What do you want?

Mr. Joseph introduced himself in his capacity as my attorney, and asked him to enter. Adnan found himself embarrassed in front of us and invited us in.

Rose appeared right behind him as we entered, so he spoke to her in French language, and she left quickly. With all contempt and shame, Adnan addressed his words to the Lawyer, saying:

-        What's the story? What's the matter, Mr.?

The Lawyer answered calmly:

-        Mr. Adnan, I am present today in front of you to solve a family dispute, the victim is an innocent child, and in my legal capacity I came to settle the matter and reach a solution that satisfies both parties.

Resentment was evident on Adnan's face, who responded by asking:

-        What is required, Sir?

With great confidence, the Lawyer told him:

-        Why don't we make a deal in the file of this crisis, and we are ready to pay the amount that you requested from my client against her release with giving back her child and her freedom. I think this solution is the most appropriate and it satisfies both parties.

Then I intervened in the negotiation, and I told him:

- Based on what you asked me previously, I collected the required amount.

The Lawyer replied with defensive attack, saying:

- Mr. Adnan, my client refused the custody claim to return her child, and preferred to avoid entering the courts since you are the father of her child. For this reason, she decided to negotiate by consensual ways to resolve the issue.

And he continued:

- Mr. Adnan, legal custody is the right of my client, as she owns the legal papers from an apartment rental contract to a work contract based on a large wage.

In the meanness of a deceitful husband, he answered the Lawyer:

- It seemed that you've prepared everything related to the file.

The lawyer replied:

- Right... We are ready to complete the case away from the Court.

Adnan thought a little, as if he was counting his money from the deal, then said:

- Well... we are in the last weeks of the school year, and the atmosphere in this period does not call for rushing so that the child may delay in his exams, so I need a short period of time to prepare him psychologically. Let me also consult a Lawyer, the matter is not that easy. After all, Kamal is my son, and I'm a dad who cares about his future.

The Lawyer replied in a firm tone:

- Believe me, Mr. Adnan, it is not in your interest to have recourse to Court, since the issue of custody is legally settled. It is better to expedite closing this file, for you will lose money and in the end, the child will be with his mother. Please decide, and I will be back tomorrow to complete the necessary procedures.

Mr. Joseph turned to me and said:

- Come on, Mrs., all you have to do is to go to the bank tomorrow to withdraw the required amount and deposit the same in the custody of Mr. Adnan.

The Lawyer extended his hand and shook hands with Adnan, who said:

- Wouldn't you like to drink something?

The Lawyer replied to him, saying:

-       Tomorrow we will drink the cup of reconciliation, hopefully, but now my client is in a hurry, and she has many things to pack and to bring the special needs for Kamal, as preparing his room and organizing his stuff that she bought for him and other tasks.

We went out of this meeting as if I were born again. I was incapable of thanking the Lawyer, and more incapable of describing the situation that overwhelmed me, to the point where I wished that the car's wheel would turn with the minutes faster to welcome tomorrow.

The Lawyer said on our return:

-       It is necessary for Adnan to feel your strength, otherwise he will not accept the principle of barter.

I replied:

-       Do you think he will agree tomorrow?

He replied:

-       Frankly, I'm a little worried since he's a deceitful man, but if he thought in it legally, he'll know it's not in his best interest to refrain or to refuse.

The Lawyer refused except to accompany me to Mrs. Suzanne's house, and it was past eight in the evening. I slowly opened the door of the house, but I was surprised by Mrs. Suzanne waiting for me and asking:

- Your delay has worried me, and I was afraid that your endeavors would have failed.

I informed her the smallest details of our meeting, and how Mr. Joseph was professional in concluding the negotiation deal with Adnan, and I am absolutely sure that my child Kamal will be in my arms soon, and that all the misfortunes that have plagued my life are gone...

Mrs. Suzanne left me to rest and entered her bedroom, while I was once again distracted by what happened and was happening to me, recalling the tape of my memories from the period when Adnan entered my life to this hour. I quietly delved into the details of his personality and psychological contract, and how a woman could bear cohabiting with an unjust man? Then I looked up at the sky, where the moon seemed to be laughing happily tonight, and the fresh air breezing longing. The image of my mother did not leave me, as her sudden departure broke my heart, so I read her verses from Quran to moisten her final resting place.

"You, who your face is a sun to my soul, don't go away from me."- Shams Tabrizi

The chirping of birds in my room balcony that morning delighted me more than any other day, just like I were on a date with life, like a lover counting minutes to meet her love of life. Suddenly, I remembered "Hajji" Um Bilal's interpretation of dreams, may God have mercy on her, when she once explained to me a dream about a child birth, saying: "My daughter, this means an anguish will be vanished". She was pious and had insight. She is always present in my heart and mind, and her advice never leave me. Some people are alive in my life but I see them as dead, and others are buried under the ground but are alive in my heart. She, may God have mercy on her, was the one who always urged me to read daily, as if she wanted me to enrich my cultural memory with learning and knowledge. Her concept was that life is an eternal school, so we must learn from it and have new experience in every single moment thereof, in which its days don't get old or tired while we walk along it toward the unknown. I became sick of this strange feeling that has pervaded my entity, as if I have forgotten all of my pains, concerns and problems, except my child's image that has dominated my thoughts, drawing the moments of life in boxes of hidden dreams, which had entangled from many sides forming a dream that tickles the feeling of every mother who had been deprived from her child.

The day was ready to crawl over my eyelids as if trying to awaken me for a new and near hope, and my chest sighs were about to reach the sky calling me to stand up, for life has regained its rhythm in this home, and family members had woken up from their beds to get ready for their school day, while I was eager for the get-together.

Mrs. Suzanne was watching me silently, which prompted her to break off her usual morning solitude with her cup of coffee, so I asked:

-       Excuse me Mrs.! I don't want to bother you.
She gave her satisfied smile, and said:

-       Never, Elham, you don't bother me, I feel the sparkle of happiness in your eyes. Come on, get rid of the monotony of days and their tragedies, and open your doors for tomorrow!

-       But happiness, Mrs. is terrifying!

With this response she took her initiative and interrupted me, saying:

-       Elham, happiness is the key to reconciliation between a person and himself, and it is the gateway to contentment and satisfaction. Happiness is believing and sticking more to our experiences, for God examines His servant to test him and to know the strength of his endurance.

I understood her words, and answered her, saying:

-        How can a mother who was deprived of her child, when he was an infant, to make up for the years of deprivation and to create trust between him and her?

She poured out of her coffee pot, perhaps the fourth cup, watched me carefully, and then replied:

-        Motherhood does not need someone to explain it, for love flows in the veins of the fetus while he was in his mother's womb. Motherhood calls us for it while we practice its rituals with love. Get up Elham, expel these obsessions out of your mind, and get ready to receive your groom... your child!

The day took me in silent labyrinths, for Life is a swing or a square crowded with faces, and every face therein is looking for a humanity maker, for the One who is able to open its closed doors of cruelty and greed, and every face is lost in the crowd of faces. Only sources of motherhood derive their being from the Lord of the worlds, while many stations on the sidewalks of life seem in a dry state, waiting the life train to pass.

What has changed today?

What has changed was that the hands of time stopped spinning, since they fell asleep at the moment of meeting when my arms became ready to embrace him. I would meet him, close my eyelids at his picture, and smell the perfume of my being from the threads of his shirt. The workshop of preparations began at home, upon Mrs. Suzanne's orders, who decided to transfer Raghad's needs and belongings to Karim's room, where Raghad's room becomes ready for my residence with my child…

I've been on pins and needles until the Lawyer arrived, so I prepared myself and went out with him, carrying five million as a ransom to get my baby back. I didn't utter a word the whole way, and the Lawyer noticed my confusion. The only thing that warmed my soul was the supplications of "Hajji" Um Bilal, may God have mercy on her, her words and her advice. I imagined her for a few seconds as if she were accompanying me to retrieve my child, a state of mumblings overwhelmed me and I felt cold, so I was afraid that the Lawyer would think I had gone crazy.

My friend realized my confusion, so he said:

- I feel how nervous you are; I can clearly see the confusion on your face...
I shyly told him:

- I'm really nervous!

He said:

- Don't worry, leave things to me, maybe Adnan will try to provoke you.

I returned to my silence and closed the door on myself as I took the first step towards the gate of freedom. As much as my life was dark, yet the light was seeping into its parts by the grace of the good people who offer the favor for free. Oh my God, how generous you are! You are the Almighty, the Most Exalted, who knows what is in the hearts. Today I will regain my freedom and forget the executioner who made my life a nightmare; I will read for the first time a new chapter of my biography.

-        Here we are??

A phrase the Lawyer uttered which brought me back to reality, so I replied:

-        Mr. Joseph, I feel like I can't walk.

He smiled pleasingly, and said:

-        Be patient, Elham, you are a great woman and a wonderful mother, your son Kamal will be proud of you one day.

We got out of the car and headed to the building. It was only moments before we knocked the door, once... twice...Then Adnan opened up straight with his angry face. He invited us to enter, hoping that we would not do that, but we insisted to set foot on the ground of his house. The Lawyer asked him if the child was ready, so he called "Rose", which made me jealous. For the first time, I felt the jealousy of the wife, the nature of love and his appreciation to her. Sometimes we become obsessed with the one we love, while his heart is beating to another woman. I looked around the place, everything was still the same: the furniture, the paintings, the photo frames that included his pictures with his African wife after he took our wedding pictures from it.

Everything was still in its place, which brought me back to the beginnings. A few minutes later, the little knight's voice shouted:

- Mom... Mom...

I opened my arms to embrace himwith a wife's pain, a mother's deprivation, and an anguish of separation... I was afraid to loosen them so that I could lose him again, for the loss had become to me a state of fear and panic. How wonderful is the fragrance of our child's breath as it penetrates our pores, connecting the arteries of the heart to each other and making the pulse different!

Adnan was suspicious and asked me:

- It seems strange, how does Kamal know that you are his mother?

I was in a state of panic, so I pulled the child to me and refused to utter a letter, while I left the Lawyer to negotiate in order to complete the deal. I caught Kamal tightly for fear that he would take him out of my arms.

The negotiation process began, and after Adnan received the money, he was relieved, as if he was selling a worthless piece of furniture. He did not realize that the deal revolved around his flesh and blood. He entered a side room and came back with a woman's bag, then said:

-        Mr. Joseph, all what Elham has is right here, this bag contains her identification papers and her passport.
The lawyer took the bag from his hand and went to check its contents. Everything was fine, from the ID card to the passport and Kamal's identity papers. As if my whole life had been imprisoned inside a small handbag, and my stolen freedom was trapped in its bottom.

After handing over and receiving, the Lawyer approached him and said:

-        Mr. Adnan, I think that we were faithful to our covenant with you, so you must be faithful with us as well. Tomorrow, on Thursday, we will meet in the Shari's Court at 10 a.m. to complete the divorce papers.

-      Divorce??

This word shook his being, and made him freeze for a moment. He was incapable of negotiating about this matter, which fell upon him like a disaster. He found himself unable to reject the idea of divorce since the Lawyer had legally restricted him.

The car took the three of us off; the Lawyer was driving slowly, while my child was laying down on my lap, embraced with my heart's great tenderness and overwhelmed with my eye's safety.

I couldn't stop the shedding of tears from my eyes, and at the same time, I was afraid to frighten the child, but the tears of joy have a special taste, since they wash away sorrows and purify the aches. At the other juncture of life, there are still unknown laughter, and things derived from happiness waiting for us. Sometimes, ends are born from beginnings, and here I am born again without fear, suspicion or dread.

I lost the words that give this Lawyer his right, and he was aware through my looks how grateful I was to him.

The only thing that was taking my time and concerning me was my child who was between my arms. From time to time, I used to glimpse a warm safety from the glow of his smile. Kamal has become a young man, with many of my features and few of his father's features, and his looks can tell deep stories of deprivation.

161

Few moments passed until we entered the safety circle or the salvation area at Mrs. Suzanne's house, this lady mother who came to me as a blessing from God in order to keep me company and save me from the pain of torment and homelessness.

The reception was full, so my tears fell upon happiness. The children were ready to welcome Kamal with their spontaneity and innocence, as for Mrs. Suzanne, who embraced the little visitor very warmly, which made him think at first that she was his aunt. After the hoopla, Mrs. Suzanne hugged him again, and asked:

-        Welcome Kamal... You are finally here, you honored us at your home, and those are your new friends who have been waiting for you impatiently.

She turned to me and said:

-        You must not give up on your determination, rather face the coming challenges with strength and persistence, as one of us does not know when adversity and difficulties will confront him. You reaped and you sowed, and here is your child between your arms, but your responsibility today is doubled, since you will be the father and the mother to him, so prove your presence on Earth.

Her words encouraged me and increased my determination to continue the path, especially when I felt a great harmony between

Kamal and the children, as if he was born and raised among them. After the noise calmed down, Mrs. Suzanne asked her two sons to bring the toys they had chosen for Kamal, so the two boys ran in each direction, and then came with the gifts, not to mention the clothes, hats and shoes she chose with her high taste. Her generosity was beyond words to thank.

I told her about what happened with us, and she asked me about the divorce file, which she considered the main focus in my case, so I told her:

-       I established a power of attorney for Mr. Joseph to authorize him to conduct a divorce application in absentia in his capacity as my legal representative. Thus, I will not see Adnan again, and Mr. Joseph has fixed the next Thursday as a date for the divorce proceedings.

She hugged me tightly and said:

-       Congratulations, Elham, you have struggled, fought and strayed for your son, and here he is between your arms. Today, sleep comfortably while he is in your bosom, and don't forget to remind the Lawyer to obtain for you a legal document that allows your child to travel with you.

"Not every fall is an end, for the rainfall is the most beautiful beginning."- Mahatma Gandhi

I am free...divorced... and a mother.

These words beautified my life with hope and brought me back to the nostalgia of past. Every time I see a smile on my child's mouth, new years sparkle inside me, for now he is far from the shackles of hate and domination. How wonderful he is while sleeping like an angel who came to guard me! I cuddle him up and watch him as if I saw him for the first time.

The night passed timidly, so I welcomed my day with a great passion and more activism. After the two boys went to school, Mrs. Suzanne came to me and asked:

-        Is Kamal ready?

I answered:

-        Yes, I will take him to his school a bit later.

I took his little warm hand, and we went out together. For the first time, his hand was in my hand and our steps were common. When we reached the courtyard, the supervisor warmly greeted us and his friends surrounded him asking about the woman who was accompanying him, so he informed them that I am his mother who was absent from him. At this moment, the Director appeared and asked me:

- Mrs. Elham, what happened?

I replied:

- I solved the problem amicably, and from today and on you will see me taking my child to your school. It was touching moments as I stood watching him entering the class with his classmates, and his eyes never leave me, for his sweet smile is the icon of my salvation…

My return to home wasin slow-motion, and my feeling was warning me of a great event, so my doubts grew and I was afraid to lose all the happiness I'm living now. I was afraid that this joy would turn into a nightmare again, knowing that I am fully aware that Adnan has become a painful memory and no longer exists in my life, and that today I am standing at another turn of life. I didn't find an explanation for all these questions that crossed my mind. As soon as I arrived, I found the lawyer waiting for me and waving with a piece of paper, so I got amazed, but I caught in Mrs. Suzanne's eyes a ray of glee, as if they had prepared a surprise for me. I came closer to them with heavy steps, asking:

- What's going on? What's wrong with you??

The Lawyer handed me the paper, and said:

-        This is your deed of liberty... This is finally your divorce paper. From now and on, you are free.

As soon as he uttered his last word, I felt very dizzy. I would have passed out if Mrs. Suzanne didn't rush to give me a glass of cold water.

I am free! How wonderful is freedom after a long dark night! My divorce paper was not the only great incidence which the Lawyer encountered me with, but there was another important thing when he put his hand in his pocket and handed me a paper stamped with legal seals, then said to me:

-        Please read the contents of this paper.

I started reading it while I was astonished, and as soon as I finished reading, I screamed loudly and my tears fell down out of my eyes, which surprised Mrs. Suzanne, so she amazingly asked the Lawyer:

-        What is the secret of this paper (Maître)?

The Lawyer turned toward her and answered:

-        This is an absolute waiver by Adnan for the custody of his son, and an authorization to facilitate travel procedures without hindrances. Finally, her case is about to end.

Frankly, I was shocked and almost embraced the Lawyer if it wasn't shameful, so I hastened to kiss the virtuous lady's hand since she stood by my side till the end of my tragedy, however, she quickly withdrew her hand, and said:

-       God forbids Elham! I've done what my conscience asked me to do, since you are a good girl and you deserve this.
I answered:

-       Um Raghad, if I sum up all the next years of my life day by day, I will not suffice you for your kindness and favor! And you, Mr. I can't find an expressive way to present my thanks and gratitude to you!
Things had changed and my day was assigned to home chores, preparing food, and taking my child to and from the school. It became necessary to think about the future and how to motivate myself to hold this responsibility. For now, I am responsible for Kamal's school and needs, as well as for upbringing and raising him to become a good man. So I had to choose between two decisions: staying and residing in the African continent or returning to my homeland. I was confused with these two options, but all what matters to me and concerns me is the future and stability of my son. I began to feel the warmth of the family when we gathered at one table, whether for lunch or dinner, while Kamal's psychological condition began to change through his presence in this family. He broke the barrier of loneliness and introversion, and launched towards a broad horizon, when every

night I narrate for him a new story from my imagination, until I thought myself a novelist of children's stories.

The days passed by at the pace of hope for a better tomorrow, until one day Mrs. Suzanne called me in her loud voice saying:

- Where are you, Elham?
- I am cleaning up Basma's room, Mrs.

She replied:

- Come here, I want to talk to you about an important issue.

Her demand concerned me, what is this important urgent issue? Does she want me to leave the house after I got my child back? The important thing is that I cheated myself and complied in front of her as she took the initiative, and said:

- Listen Elham, tomorrow Bilal and his brother Mazen will arrive from Lebanon, so I thought that you would move with Kamal to "Hajji" Um Bilal's apartment, may God have mercy on her, so that you would be comfortable with your son, but during the day you will be here with us. What do you think?

I hugged her tightly and said:

- Tell me how could I thank a great lady just like you!

Her decision was right, since the apartment would be small for all of us, and I will not be comfortable with Kamal. In addition, all my dreams, struggles and sorrows are in that house, and there where my struggle for freedom had begun. O God, how great your favor is, for you chose for me this kind and nice family.

Indeed, I moved with Kamal at night to the house of this pure "Hajji", may God have mercy on her. The house was missing the scent of the compassionate woman, so it seemed sorrowful for her departure; even her stick nudge was silent. Kamal was curious about the place, so he started inquiring a lot, and I was tired of finding the satisfying answers that would please his curiosity, as if I was always just keen to reveal my love for him. How couldn't be, for he is the sun and the shadow of my life?

"O Friendship, without you one would be alone, and by your grace one can multiply himself and live in the souls of others."
Voltaire

Finally, the school year has ended and we decided to return to the homeland; so the Lawyer quickly finished all the necessary legal documents and procedures to facilitate our travel. He obtained a passport for my son, and we booked two non-return flight visas. Life appeared to me in mysterious and unclear colors, particularly, as I bear the responsibility of a child who will later approach adolescence and youth, to end afterwards a period of suffering and torment.

I was counting the last hours in confusion... The night of departure, and before heading to the Airport, I sat behind the glass of the window that overlooks the street, while my child next to me was in a deep sleep, and I repeated the tape of memories, the day I came to this African country as a bride seeking happiness within the house of her groom, and looking towards tomorrow with an optimistic spirit. I was a naive woman at that time, who lived dreams as reality, and got sick by a cold breeze when it passed towards her. I was ignorant of the tricks and ploys of life, as if I were a sheep that was led to slaughter by her will. The things around me were strange, even the sky here was very different from that in my homeland, filled with tragedies and poverty, contrary to our joyful and laughing skies, for people here are different from the people in my country. Their faces were gloomy, covered with masks that hide feelings. The wails of being abroad were squeezing my tired heart, and the longing to fly to Beirut overwhelmed me. I missed the breeze of the homeland and the faces therein... I missed my brothers, my father and the places that became from the past in my tired memory. Silence at these moments was my ecstasy till drunkenness, to the point where I thought a fairy had come to stay up with me and to amuse me, and the spaces of place and time no longer frightened me. The coming days under the sky of my country are able to heal wounds. At that moment, I painted pictures of virtual people in my memory, I smiled at them and drowned in their laughter.

While being obsessed in these plenty of feelings, I glanced at my child Kamal and saw him sleeping peacefully and silently, wearing on his eyes an indescribable innocence. It was a touching scene and a tearful look. I am the one who sacrificed my life, spent my youth for many days at people's homes while serving them, and endured humiliation and insult in order to retrieve the trust that was once estranged from me.

As I was wandering in this farewell moment through the journey of memories, I recalled the events of my marriage or the clauses of the deal that I was its victim. They were painful and exhausting, as if I was reading a script for a cinematic story, especially since Adnan practiced the ugliest power over me, as he deprived me of safety and hacked my dreams and feelings. He humiliated me, insulted me and bargained with me, but for a moment, he forgot that he was the victim of his bitter truth from which he was fleeing into the arms of hatred. He was poor and pitiful.

This is my last night in this country. I must be asleep in my bed, since my flight takes off at five in the morning, but my obsessions and these feelings raging inside me robbed sleepiness from me.

Now I am turning a bitter page from the chapter of my life so far, a page that I have only read its main title written in letters of oppression and deprivation. Unexpectedly, the image of Mrs. Reem, who received me at her home, appeared before me, and then the image of Mrs. Hind, who had wronged me, so I felt senses of injustice in my heart and fires that burns the "debris" of my days. My life is like a broken glass...Oh life! What shall I overcome more? My misery or the harshness of my days? I am afraid that the air will blow and cause my heart to fall with the love that it holds for my son, for there is nothing left in me after my crash! This is the last time I watch my heartburn, and this is the last burnt breath inside of me. It just happened and we're done with it!

The fire of rebellion raged within me, perhaps to revenge against fate!

I am now more satisfied if I tell Mrs. Hind the truth about her husband and the reason behind escaping from serving at her home. It is necessary to tell her what had happened. I will be in another place, far from her. I would never forget her face as she bid me farewell after she knew the truth when I told her:

-       Mrs. Hind, blind trust even in the closest people to us is the short way to betrayal.
I would bid farewell to her with this phrase that I should have realized it and knew its meaning the moment I got married to Adnan. Blind trust is the sword that cuts the bond of the emotional relationship.

The sleepiness refused to touch my eyelids, and the scribbles of dawn appeared before me, just like threads of light on the verge of dawning. It's three in the morning, my bags are at the door, the taxi is waiting for us outside, and Kamal has woken up.

The farewell moments were touching, especially when I noticed the tears in Mrs. Suzanne's eyes and I felt the parting blow when children cuddled each other. I hugged her tightly, so she approached my ear, and said:

-      Good-bye, Elham, tomorrow evening you will be among your family and your people, you will be freed from the prison, but I will always remember you since you were "a prisoner behind the bars of time." Live the life, fly in the sky of feelings and do not let fate deceive and defeat you again.

I dreaded looking back, so as not to be defeated by my tears and to be weakened again. I surrendered to the Lord of the worlds, then the car drove towards the next of the near future, while my little heart was playing songs of hope and my hand was holding the hand for whom I gave my life.

Kamal's questions increased and I was unable to find answers to some of them, until we get on the plane. I caught a glimpse of fear in his eyes, which confused me. I said to him:

-      I want you as a man, Kamal, and real men never have fear.

Then I dropped the last look out of the plane's window at a country which stole from me happiness, as I strayed in its streets begging for mercy and tenderness, slept in the outdoors, and cried until the tears have been sick of me.

The plane flew for many hours while we were strangers on board, cruising over the cities in a capacious space. At nine p.m., after a flight that lasted about sixteen hours, I glimpsed Beirut from my window, it was like a sparkling bride adorned with ruby, and its night was quiet and calm. A heavy tear dropped from my eyes with burning bitterness, due to the plane landing, the crowding at the customs center, the good reception, and the emptiness of the arrivals hall from those I wished to see among the faces.

My steps were heavy and my hands were trembling. I looked away again; perhaps I could glimpse her face, touch it, and please my eyes with it. However, now she sees me from above and feeling satisfied about me, since I neither defied nor disobeyed her orders. Mom, who your face has exceeded all faces.

My father... I glimpsed him from afar holding a bunch of white roses in his hand... I broke through the rows; opened my hands and fell into his arms sniffing his scent...His wife stood beside him looking surprisingly at me. Then, I turned towards my brothers and hugged them one by one, while my father came closer and embraced Kamal, who seemed surprised by what was going on around him. Nabil was among the recipients... Oh, Nabil, my cousin! I recognized him from the mole on his cheek.

He didn't change; he is still handsome, full of masculinity, of light brown skin, and tall. I greeted him warmly since we haven't met for a long time, due to my migration to the African continent, which deprived me of all my family and relatives... Oh, Mrs. Rana...I forgot all the faces except hers, she was the brightest when she hugged me warmly and said:

- Finally, Elham, thank God for your safety.

Tears fell on my cheeks, and I replied with a slaughtered voice:

- Mrs. Rana, I will never forget your kindness to me throughout my life. May God have mercy on "Hajji", she was my mother and all my life, and may God reward Mrs. Suzanne for all her favors!

Mrs. Rana wiped my tears and said:

- Today you will be my guest for an urgent matter, and I apologized to your father, since there is a testament that I must pass on to you alone.

Terror beats hit my heart, and then I surprisingly asked her:

- A testament?

Yes, she nodded.

After taking Kamal to the guest room to sleep peacefully, Mrs. Rana invited me to sit with her in the evening-room. She was at first confused, but then she was encouraged and said:

\-   Look Elham, "Hajji" recommended me the day I visited you, before coming to Lebanon, to protect and support you if something happened to her. As you know I don't have a sister, but I consider you a one.

I interrupted her saying:

\-   I swear I feel the same way towards you.

She sighed and said:

\-   So, Hajji's testament was to live with your child in her house located in Ghobeiri. The apartment has been closed and abandoned for a long time, and from next Monday you will start working with me in the company.

Words lost silently on my lips.

I began to send mercy upon her, and prayed for the long-life of Mrs. Rana among her family.

"Love is the only way out of non-existence into existence." - Platon

This is life...

But it is a new life for me, everything has become organized therein, my daily tasks, my responsibilities, my relationship with Kamal, and the most important thing is his education. I specified a day for us to go to restaurants or parks together, and I always told him that his father was a good person who loved him very much. I started a different life than I had before.

Long weeks passed while I was plunging in my thoughts. Life took me there occasionally, and I wondered why Nabil is trying to be so close to me? Am I able to open a new vent to the heart? Sometimes I regret avoiding him, and I secretly say: This relationship must be on a clear track.

I lived a difficult psychological conflict within me, for I was not able to have a man other than Kamal in my life, he was all my life. But in the other hand, I began to consider that I am entitled to continue with a person who loves and respects me, who will compensate me for what I have suffered and grieved. Having Nabil by my side was promising for a new beginning in my life. I used to meet him in front of the company at my time to go, asking me to drive me home. I was feeling his confusion, his resentment and anger at me for being indifferent towards him.

This dilemma continued until one day Mrs. Rana noticed his insisting, interest, and strong desire to be with me. She advised me to think twice so that I would not regret missing the opportunity.

One day, work was exhausting, and I was alone in the office, waiting the end of the day. While I was thinking about the gift my father gave to Kamal, I fell into a deep sleep that soon turned into a terrifying nightmare! I saw faces coming towards me, gloomy, dark... My heart cramped... This is our neighbor Abu Mohamad and his son... What brought them here? I asked them:

- What happened, Abu Muhammad? Did anything happen to my father?
He replied with gloomy eyes:
- Come with us.
Then he muttered talking to himself: There is neither might nor power except with God.

I lost my feelings and I didn't understand anything, but his son continued, saying:

-     Kamal is in the hospital. He was hit by a car while he was riding his bicycle in the street.

I got stuck in my place like I lost my senses for a moment; I didn't know how to act. I felt that my feet weren't helping, and I couldn't stand anymore. Hasn't time had enough of causing me pains and calamities? Then a young man came from the company and helped me; I dragged my feet, and the shoes slipped from them...

I ran barefoot not knowing where to go. I rubbed my hands, hoping a mercy from the inhabitant of heaven.

I was heartbroken, downhearted, the world faced me in its blackness, surrounded me with fear from every direction, and the neighing of the wind penetrated my ears as if it were the hum of bullets.

I arrived to the hospital, and found my father in the lobby. He was pale, I approached him, but he turned away from me. I lost my mind, then I caught his shirt and pulled him violently perhaps he utters a word, but he didn't, instead, his tears were pouring out from his eyes profusely. I started to turn around myself to find someone who could guide me to Kamal. However, the faces disappeared, the bodies became eyeless, and I didn't find an explanation of what was happening.

I cried out loudly:

-        Kamaaaaaaaaaaaal, where are you, my life?

The echo was silent, and I ran in a hurry towards the reception to ask about him, where a voice of one of them came from behind and said:

-        Mercy be upon him! He became a bird in heaven…

I was in a state of whining; I started pulling my hair unaware of what was happening around me, and screamed as loud as I could:

-         Let me see him! O Deceivers, I'm sure he's waiting for me! It is impossible for him to leave me and go alone. Where is my son?

My father hugged me and said:

-         There is neither might nor power except with God, may God give us patience during our ordeal.

The letters disappeared, the echo of the voice was cut off, and the universe stopped spinning, so I asked him:

-         How did this happen?

My father said, with a heartbreak:

-         He was getting out of the alley facing the main street on his bike, while speeding...

I unconsciously ran to the road barefoot, so my feet were bled by the pebbles. I wasn't feeling any pain, for my heart ache was greater than all the aches. I started to search in the place of the accident to track his trace that disappeared, but I didn't find him. I searched for him in my bosom, but I find it empty. Has Kamal become an illusion???

I controlled myself and overcame my tears, but I realized certainly it was the truth! A burning fire washed over me and the world turned around me without stopping, then a tremor shocked my body, so that the space was filled by screaming due to my pain and sadness. I tried to open my eyes perhaps I could find him hiding inside of them. I prostrated near the blowing smell of his body, but I didn't find him, I found nothing except emptiness... Kamal passed away!!!

I screamed with non-stop:

Come back to me, Kamal! Give me a favor and return to my soul, return to the vaults of my days, Mom! Don't leave me alone, heartbroken and tormented! Take off the robe of death and come back or take me with you! They stole your life from me at the turning point! I am sick, Mom, due to my pain and need for you! For whom do you leave me? My senses flooded the face of Earth until I surrendered myself to heaven.

If fate could speak, it would have told us that it cheated by giving us the dreams that it allows us to see! Even our dreams were sadistic, just like our circumstances; we live their details as if misery and death come out thereof.

I burst into tears like a child until my breath choked and I could no longer hold it, to open my eyes to see Nabil, who was trying to wake me up from the worst nightmare I had lived for a minutes and which had nothing to do with reality, taking me home and whispering:

\-   Come here Elham, Kamal is waiting for us; I will show you another dawn from my wide window!

The dream scattered in the light of the day and finally drew a smile, so I realized the fact that the future will bring me an endless beautiful dream, and the fate will finally grant me the sweetness of life, as the days of sorrow shall end. I missed drawing happiness on my face, is it reasonable for the heart to be damaged by a lot of rust?!

Nabil is the city that I have not visited yet, which opens the doors for me in order to walk into its streets after all those distorted days, suffocated in the maze of injustice. I will wake up from my ruined days, to get back to the ancient and old times of the past; leaning on the stick of Nabil's love and heart beating, after the chords of eagerness got tired and dried up.

I will retrieve myself back and tear the shroud of the bygone days. I will never go back to the tortuous roads since they no longer belong to me... Sadness no longer distracts me, and the dream has become a reality!

Nabil, you are the delayed joy... I will never be sad again! I may have finally woken up from my tomb!

Done

The Novelist Zeina Jradi

The gate of feeling remains closed until the word is unleashed…

There is a bridge adorned with emotions and transparency that connects it with the reader...

A novelist, a writer and a media person who developed the word to be used towards the world of imagination, so that she created the heroes of her novels using imagination and considered them as real people. Her good friend is the book, for she is a diligent guest at book exhibitions, and she is an active participant in cultural seminars and conferences.

Zeina Jradi began her creative career at an early age. She was an avid reader of the novels of Ihsan Abdel Koddous and Najib Mahfouz, and sometimes moved between: Asia Jabbar, Nawal Al Saadawi, Hanan Al Sheikh and many others.

Her first step in writing was in the print media, where she worked as a journalist and editor in several Lebanese and Arab newspapers and publications, then she carried out correspondence tasks at Dar Al Sada, and then she became an owner of many publications, including:

Magazine:

- Sanaa

- ESTHETIC

-BELLA TEENAGER

She distributed her media activity in all media categories. She had a distinguished presence in several television stations in the visual media. She also prepared many television programs and held the office of the general manager in the company of:

DIVA PRODUCTION for art production.

She wrote art, social sciences, culture, politics, article, and art of analysis and dialogue, which formed a vibrant cultural knowledge in her memory.

Zeina Jradi got into the world of " novels" through her novel "A Prisoner behind the Bars of Time", embodying the suffering of oppressed motherhood in the context of her novel events with a delicate sense.

She is preparing to publish the following books:

-       A Woman's Scribbles: Feelings arising from typical reality of life.

- In the Presence of Destiny: An emotional novel inspired by the world of espionage.
- Dancing in the Devil's Temple: A novel of a deeply ideological, emotional and human nature.

Zeina carried a heart that cares about the human pain in our Arab homeland. Her pen was transparently depicting this pain, highlighting the issues that concern us and affect our reality in our societies in the Arab world.

Made in United States
Orlando, FL
13 August 2022

20964626R00117